Amy Taylor Cook has been an aspiring author since she could hold a pen. Her debut novel *Sometime in August* is based partly on her own experiences with mental health, and it aims to discuss the topic in a blunt and relatable manner.

Amy grew up in East Kilbride, Greater Glasgow, where she currently lives with her fiancé along with pet snails and a huge collection of books.

To my family, friends and, most importantly, John, for putting up with me all this time.

Amy Taylor Cook

SOMETIME IN AUGUST

AUSTIN MACAULEY PUBLISHERS™

LONDON · CAMBRIDGE · NEW YORK · SHARJAH

A CIP catalogue record for this title is available from the British Library.

ISBN 9781398441446 (Paperback)
ISBN 9781398441453 (ePub e-book)

www.austinmacauley.com

First Published 2023
Austin Macauley Publishers Ltd®
1 Canada Square
Canary Wharf
London
E14 5AA

Most importantly, to my fiancé, John. You have given me years of joy, and saved me in so many ways. I look forward to every single day that comes when I am with you. I can't wait for a future full of dogs, travelling and lie-ins.

To my parents, Lee and John, for years upon years of great advice, unconditional support and for always being proud of me. And to Ian, Scott and my grandparents for being the greatest set of people to grow up with. And to the entirety of my fiancé's family; a family I am privileged to become a part of.

Friday

6:00am. *Fucking hell. Why was I awake?*

I blinked furiously at my phone screen, locking it as if to convince myself I hadn't seen the time, but the sudden brightness left irritating flashes of light, even when I shut my eyes. I rolled over, pulled the covers under my chin, and stared at the wall, studying it. It was white, albeit faded, after years of it being a hotel room. I counted the raised dots that looked like braille and wondered what fluids that wall had been met with over the years. I shuddered at the thought and rolled back to face the window.

The curtains were shut, but the late summer light was already creeping through as they danced slightly to the breeze that was blowing in. A river ran past the front of my hotel, and if I concentrated hard enough, I could just about make out the gentle trickle of water passing. The sound, however, was soon drowned out by the noise of early morning commuters; cars cruising by, rushed footsteps and the rolling of bikes. I took in the peaceful ambience whilst I could. This extra hour of undisturbed stillness as the world woke up was one benefit of my insomnia.

The other students, spread across different rooms within the hotel, were likely still asleep and wouldn't be rising for another hour or so. We had been together for a week, studying for college, and were due to be here next week too. Our course was small, with only thirteen of us – all studying media – but we were based across Britain. We had three Scotsmen (one of them being me), an Irishman and a Welshman, with the other eight coming from various parts of England. We sounded like the start of a very bad 'walking into a bar' joke.

Their company, whilst fun, could be too much sometimes, especially when I was seeing them all day, every day. I was acutely aware they all felt the same at some point or another and you would when you lose that much personal time. So that brief window of time when you first wake up or before going to bed was treasured amongst us. And stopped us from ripping each other's heads off.

I felt some relief that they would all be returning home for the weekend. I wouldn't be; my home was six hundred miles away, back in Scotland. So I would be moving hotels that night, staying in a different one from our usual, and spending a weekend alone. Well, maybe a bit longer than the weekend, after what I had planned for tonight. My two fellow Scotsmen weren't travelling back either, however, unlike me, they were staying at the houses of others. I did not have that luxury – nor did I want it, frankly. It would have gotten in the way of my plans.

My phone buzzed and I jumped with surprise, wondering who was up this early suffering alongside me. It was merely an email notification from some shop I ordered something from months ago, screaming at me about their latest sale. I deleted it without even opening it, and decided to give into my responsibilities for the day and swung my legs over the side of the bed, resigning to getting up.

The early-morning chill hit my skin, but it wasn't unwelcomed. England has been uncharacteristically warm; I had spent the whole week sweating, and it would likely continue on as the day picked up. I wandered into the bathroom, and ran some tap water over my face, before examining myself in the mirror.

I don't allow many people to see me without make-up on. On my worst days, I've likened myself to an ogre, and on my better days, I would probably say I was 'sort of' cute if you squinted and looked hard enough. My face was round, and pudgy, with a nose that looked somewhat fine head-on, but had a bump in the middle if you looked at me from the side. My eyes, whilst a pleasant enough hazel colour, were too small and close together and were always coupled with dark bags under my eyes (which at this point seemed permanent). My lips were shaped nicely but when I smiled, I looked pained. My eyebrows were a product of furious plucking, as I had a monobrow until I was thirteen and since then, been dreadfully worried about the return of a single hair on my face.

That didn't even begin to cover my list of insecurities, which ranged from my stretch marks to my chubby stomach, to my flat ass. But, if I were to sit and detail everything I disliked about myself, I would have no time left in the day. So I poured out my make-up and applied it like it was my armour, following the same pattern I had done for years; primer, foundation, concealer, power, contour, highlight, eyebrows, eyeshadow, eyeliner, mascara and, finally, false lashes: my staple piece.

Anything I dared to like about myself was man-made. I had my make-up, which I plastered on daily, to an admittedly obsessive level. I also had my piercings and tattoos. If I couldn't be naturally beautiful, like so many of my friends, I would simply modify myself with art I loved.

I examined myself one more time in the mirror, before getting dressed. I would never look different again; this is how I would be immortalised, at age twenty. The Heather that looked back at me in my reflection would be the last version of her that anyone saw. I would be going out with my signature black liner and false lashes.

I dressed and packed my suitcase, ready to take it to my next hotel after the day's training. At least, I thought it was a half-day, and we would finish at noon. For now, however, I had some time before I had to wander downstairs for breakfast. I sat on the leather armchair under the window, propped my feet up on the windowsill, and watched the river and willow trees for what seemed like an age.

I wasn't much of an eater this early in the morning, so when I slid into my seat in the middle of the table, I simply watched as my colleagues ate breakfast and chatted. I sat in between Kai and Jamie, and across from Ethan (who took great pleasure in lovingly mocking me as I sat down, as only good friends can do). They were as cheerful and lively as a group of 20-something year-olds could be at 8 am, when they faced a half-day of lectures and a long trip home afterwards.

I made a general, meaningless chat with them, and no one appeared to think anything different about my demeanour, which relieved me. But the food and morning catch-up didn't last long as we all soon piled out of the hotel, throwing our luggage into car boots, and making the fifteen-minute drive to work, all of us split between five cars.

I called shotgun in Olivia's bright yellow car, lovingly nicknamed, *Bee*. With Graham in the back, the three of us moved on.

The drive to college was, admittedly, stunning. The country road follows the river, as the trees were bending over, almost kissing the ground with their leaves. For the right person, it would be poetic. But today, for me, I simply couldn't appreciate it. Luckily, I didn't have to fill the silence with any attempt at conversation. With Graham in the back seat, no one really needed to talk, as he let out a stream of near-constant commentary. You couldn't help but like him, in a sort of 'annoying younger sibling' manner.

The building we studied in was in a nice area, on the outskirts of a forest. Today wasn't going to be hands-on, or exciting, as we were scheduled for a three-hour lecture on some topic that had escaped my mind long ago. Computers, maybe? Something technical, at least.

I was away from my thoughts, in my own personal bubble, and barely registered the process of getting from the car to my seat in our lecture room. Nonetheless, there I was, in between Olivia and Connor. Our lecturer was a nice enough gentleman, whose name I forgot in my current haze. He was someone we had met a handful of times before, with a speciality in engineering. Or at least, I think it was engineering. To be honest, he could have said anything that day and I would not have taken it in. My head was elsewhere, imagining future scenarios over and over, playing out every possible outcome meticulously, whilst I anxiously bounced my leg.

If anyone had noticed my mental sabbatical, they didn't mention it. Although, I'm sure they were all just trying to survive a Friday morning lecture. Compulsive daydreaming served me well, and the morning seemed to be over within seconds; much like I was sleeping. Which I would, in theory, be doing a lot of after today.

We gathered outside post-lecture, almost in a limbo of what to do. Most of us didn't have anywhere in particular to rush back to, bar Graham who had a flight to make, so Connor suggested lunch.

Much like the journey to work, the journey back to town went by without much notice from myself, bar when Olivia pulled over to let me check into the new hotel I would be at over the weekend. Or, at least, just for tonight. Depending on when I was found. I needed to stop thinking about life past tonight.

Regardless, I didn't get to look at the room too much as I didn't want to keep everyone wanting, so I just threw my bags in and shut the door behind me. I'd have plenty of time to look later, anyway.

That's how we found ourselves gathered on the rooftop of a local pub. As I had suspected, the sun was beating down on us, so I was grateful for the ice-cold vodka coke I was very unattractively wolfing down. The rooftop was beautiful and peaceful; decorated with flowers and hanging pots, and the tables aligned with couches and soft seats, rather than typical bar stools. We were the only ones there, all locked away in our own part of the world for that afternoon.

I considered those who were surrounding me, all momentarily caught up in studying their phones or examining the menu. I sat on the corner couch, legs stretched out, claiming what was easily about three spaces to myself. But no one seemed to mind. To my right was Alistair, followed by

Jamie and Kai. On the other side sat Connor, Olivia, Ruaridh and Ethan. I truly adored each of them. And Graham, of course, whose absence was noticeable as everything seemed much quieter without his voice.

We were, frankly, a forced friend group; anyone could see that. We were all chosen for this course, and consequently, immediately began spending a lot of time as a close group. I've always been of the opinion that if we met in any other circumstance, we likely would not be friends. There were a lot of conflicting personalities and types of people here. However, we grew together and all our eccentricities and mixed-up backgrounds played together, and everyone seemed to fit into this weird circle. Well, everyone except me, of course.

I watched Ethan stand up, and head downstairs to place an order. Ethan was a fellow Scotsman, and I loved him more than I cared to admit. Our friendship was based on ripping the piss out of each other, and we both took pleasure in proclaiming fake hatred for each other. All our playful torment was just thinly veiling our mutual love. I had the utmost respect for Ethan. He was smart, determined, and had all the great qualities you would find in someone destined to succeed, which made me a little bitter that I wouldn't be around to see it.

My gaze drifted to Ruaridh, the cocky Welshman. He was like marmite; either you loved him, or he was completely unbearable. I like to think he knew this, and didn't really care either. He had a way with the ladies and always seemed to be bragging about some 'conquest' (although I'm sure there were always some hints of exaggeration in his stories). Despite this, he was truly sweet, in his own, weird, Ruaridh, way. He was great fun and knew exactly what he wanted from life, which isn't true for a lot of people. He was marmite, for sure, but I liked marmite.

Olivia was beside him, fixing her hair with my brush that she always seemed to borrow. She was classically stunning, with an equally wonderful personality. She was soft-spoken but hit out with some brilliant humour, which was perhaps added to by her delicate voice. She was a few years older than me, but it didn't matter at all; we were close, and I valued her immensely. If I didn't love her so much, I'd have hated her out of pure envy; like one of those girls in high school who was leagues above you in the popularity charts.

I watched Olivia's neighbour Connor take a drink and inwardly smiled. I had instantly liked Connor when I first met him, and that may have been partly due to his striking resemblance to Jake, my boyfriend. In both appearance and mannerisms, they were similar, and in an odd way, this made me feel comfortable around him as if I could find part of Jake within him. He was one of the older ones in our mix-matched group, and I had genuinely yet to hear someone say a bad word against him.

As Ethan returned with a drink, I turned my attention to Alistair on my right. Alistair was one of those rare few people who was, quite simply, a good person. He was laid-back, contributing to conversations only when he felt he had something to add, whether it be funny or useful. He was kind to a fault, avoided any colleague dramas, and always seemed happy to just be about. His presence was familiar, comforting and pleasing.

As I watched Jamie, next to Alistair, he noticed me and jokingly grimaced. I laughed as he looked back down at his phone. We had the same sort of friendship as Ethan and I; love disguised as playful banter. And just like Ethan, Jamie was one of those people I knew would go far. A lot of what we studied came very naturally to him, and he was flourishing. Despite my jealousy, I was pleased for him, as a friend should be.

Kai completed our table. She was fantastically wild; with short, bright blue hair and a fierce personality, I adored how true to herself she was. She made no apologies for anything, you took her as she was, or not at all. She was incredibly admirable as a result and I wish I had a shred of her courage and 'fuck you' attitude.

I had never truly taken the time to think about each of them as in-depth as I did in that moment. But I was overcome with what felt somewhat like nostalgic feelings, and I felt desperate to soak up everything I loved about them before they left. They were good people, and I could only hope that my future actions would ultimately make them happier. I had to tell myself that they would. Otherwise, what was I doing this for?

I winced a little as my internal monologue sounded quite cringy. My observations, if written down, would read like the start of a play; quick character explanations for the actors before they began their scene.

I picked at a cheese toastie I didn't really want, but ordered as to not raise suspicion, and nursed a few more drinks whilst I observed the group. I didn't take note of what was being said, I simply watched, like a television on mute. I took my time to absorb the little things; the sun rays bouncing off Olivia's earrings and Ruaridh's watch, Connor's head thrown back in laughter as he clapped his hands together,

Kai's thumbs bouncing off her phone screen as she texted her girlfriend.

My thoughts drifted back to my friends at home, in Scotland. I couldn't entirely remember the last time I saw them (Was it at the pub? Most likely knowing us.) and I realised, bitterly, that I would not be able to take the chance to just sit and watch them like I am doing now.

I smirked into my glass as I raised it to my lips and thought about what we jokingly called ourselves, *the Struggle*. This was based on a comment Sam made years before about life being *an absolute wee struggle*. Which was a statement that ran painfully true, particularly today.

I joined the Struggle when I began dating Jake, three-and-a-half years ago, and I quickly settled in. Whilst I was content on my rooftop bar, under the English sun, with a group of bizarrely brilliant people, I would have given anything for the Struggle to be there too. To look up and see the smiling faces of Sam, Ben, Ryan, and Gaby one last time.

And Jake, my boyfriend.

I slammed my empty glass onto the table with some force, drawing eyes onto me.

"Watch yourselves, everyone, Heather's had a *single* breath of alcohol, that's her gone! She's pissed!" Ethan threw his hands up in mock fear. I flipped him off as everyone else laughed. My status as a lightweight was well known to anyone who had ever seen me drink.

However, my college friends were lucky as I had never truly unleashed the full power of 'drunk Heather' and her bad influence around them. They were fortunate, indeed, that they lived so far away and had never attended one of my house parties, as a 'Heather house party' was certainly a spectacle to behold.

I had hosted Jake's 18th birthday party a few years ago, saying that it deserved to be something huge. I regretted that statement later on. After our usual crowd of friends came over, I simply stopped counting who was coming in. There were too many people; colleagues, friends of friends, and partners of invited guests. That's likely what set everything else into motion.

I remembered waking up the next morning, lying in my parents' bed with Jake and Sam. Someone was lying on the floor, sleeping in their entire party outfit, shoes included. To go downstairs, you'd have found Ben sleeping on one couch, with someone's unidentifiable plus one on the other, and Ryan rolled up on the living room rug, fast asleep.

As I sat, nursing a hangover from hell, I was reminded by my similarly suffering guests what had happened the previous night, and I simply refused to believe it at first.

Ben had begun by telling me that Sam had jokingly punched him in the stomach a bit too hard, leading to Ben then vomiting over my bedroom, which, incidentally, was where I had been telling visitors to put their coats and bags. So they were, of course, covered in his dinner.

After this, Ben had stumbled into my parents' room, to open the window and hang out of it, getting some much-needed fresh air. This is when, however, he proceeded to empty more stomach contents out the window and down the side of the house.

In the upstairs hallway, Ryan had apparently been found with an electric power drill, screwing a torn-off door handle back into place. We never did discover who had managed to rip off said door handle in an extraordinary display of drunken strength, or how Ryan had managed to find my father's toolbox.

Downstairs, we had people spewing in the kitchen sink, downstairs bathroom, and in the front and back gardens at a somewhat impressive rate.

We also discovered £45 missing from Gaby's purse, and although we had some suspects, we never managed to figure out who it was. However, we trusted that it wouldn't be someone from our immediate friend group, but rather from the outer circle of people that were continually appearing throughout the night at an alarming rate.

We had regretted kisses, gate crashers, and arguments. The washing machine flooded onto the kitchen floor after an attempt to wash bile-soaked clothes went wrong, and the perpetrator failed to close the door properly. Said perpetrator being me.

As the party died down, and people began to head home, Sam stumbled into my parents' room to sleep, and fell over, accidentally tripping and knocking over their television. He also took down a framed photo of my family in the process, breaking the glass. When Jake and I had attempted to retire to bed, we found Sam still asleep. We didn't have the heart to move him and just settled down next to him.

Jake also later informed me that Ben had tempted me with pizza. Which, normally, would not be a particularly noteworthy exchange. However, I live in a vegetarian household and have been raised vegetarian since birth. By that point, I had never even tasted meat before. And it was a pepperoni pizza.

Jake had been particularly maddened by Ben pushing me to eat it, and I was simply happy I didn't remember the taste. Regardless, the entire night became one of many fond and hilarious alcohol-fuelled memories we shared. I wasn't sure if my house was a catalyst for drunken insanity, or if my friend group was somewhat feral. Perhaps both? It was a dangerous combination.

I had tried my best to hide the party from my parents, but in my rush to perfect the house, I missed a single slice of pizza that had made its way under their bed, and I was caught out. Despite that, Heather-hosed house parties had become a tradition whenever my parents went on a holiday.

I glanced at my current gathering of friends and realised they would probably never have memories with me like that.

"What time is it?" Olivia asked, her voice breaking my daydream.

"Eh, about two." Connor checked his phone.

"Should we get going?" Ethan turned to Kai. He was to be staying at hers for the weekend.

Kai nodded, and it seemed like everyone was packing up, getting ready to go. I was in no particular rush, but stood up and stretched.

"Olivia, any chance of dropping me off at the shops as you're driving out?" I asked.

"The things I do for you," she joked, whilst sarcastically shaking her head and rolling her eyes.

Outside, we tossed a couple of parting goodbyes as people jumped into cars and began to push off. I tried to give as casual a goodbye to them as I felt capable of at the moment. *Remember, Heather, pretend nothing is wrong.*

I slid back into the front seat of Olivia's Bee for the third time today, and the last time ever.

"What are you going to do this weekend?" she asked, looking out the rear view window as she reversed.

I shrugged. "Going to the shops, buying food, walking back to the hotel and having a lazy night tonight. Then I'll probably wander about the town, see what it is like at a weekend."

I laughed a little, whether it be at my own audacious lying or Olivia's sudden exclamation, "But you're going to be so bored!"

"Honestly, I'm looking forward to some alone time," I admitted. At least that part wasn't a lie.

The drive wasn't long, thankfully; it was just a trundle down the main street road. Olivia filled up the time telling me about how excited she was for her BBQ tonight with her friends, and her hopes she wouldn't be too tired to enjoy it. She also wasn't sure if she would go to her dad's or not afterwards.

I smiled and nodded, and yet the only thing going through my head was, *you'll be busy tonight. Good.*

She pulled into the car park, I hopped out with my bag over my shoulder and leaned down to throw a thank you and goodbye into her window. She beamed at me.

I didn't even watch her drive off, in her bright yellow run-around with a Pikachu decal on the back window. If I stood and watched her turn the corner, I don't know how long I would have continued to stand there for; staring at the empty spot on the road.

I simply marched straight into the store.

First shop: Children's stationery set.
Second shop: Matches.
Third shop: Two litres of alcohol.

I stood on the bridge that separated the main street from the quieter side of town, where both my previous hotel and current hotel sat. My bag, coupled with a blue plastic bag full of my purchases, sat at my feet. The river was much wider than the view from the window this morning suggested, and as I leaned over the brick walls and looked down, I thought about how 6 am seemed like a lifetime ago. I followed a small family of ducks as they paddled aimlessly under the bridge and out of view; probably as desperate to get out of the heat as I was.

I was sticking to myself with sweat, and as I raised the back of my hand to wipe my forehead, I felt my hair glue to myself. I was desperate to soak in an ice-cold shower, but I wasn't ready to leave the spot where I stood quite yet. I pulled my phone out of the back pocket of my shorts and dialled.

Three rings, then, "Hello?"

"Hi, Grandpa, it's Heather!"

"Oh hello! Jan, it's your wonderful granddaughter!" My grandpa's voice rose with delight when he heard me on the phone, and I heard my gran in the background laugh as my grandpa addressed her.

My grandparents and I were incredibly close. They were my dad's parents, and as my mum's parents had passed before I was old enough to truly remember them, all my love as a grandchild was poured onto them.

I adored the story of my gran and grandpa's first date, which was fortunate as my grandpa recited it for me whenever

23

I visited them. I'm not sure if he always forgot I already knew, or if he simply loved recalling that memory, but regardless, I was happy to sit back and hear it time and time again.

They had taken the train to Wemyss Bay, a stunning coastline village, before getting a ferry to Rothesay. They spent the day there, simply getting to know each other whilst exploring the town.

On their walk back to the port, they saw a ferry leaving. My grandpa had chosen this moment to joke that they had missed the last ferry, which ironically, they actually had. With very little money, they could not afford a hotel room for the night. So throughout the night, they wandered before settling in a bus stop and sharing a bag of chips; eventually managing to get the 6 am ferry.

"How are you?" I asked, and I couldn't help but smile a big, toothy smile. I simply adored my grandparents, and they were certainly always pleased to hear from me.

"All the better for speaking to you," my grandpa replied, as he always did, before asking, "would you like to speak to Gran?"

"Yes, please!"

My grandpa was hard of hearing, and it was typically easier to just speak directly to my gran rather than fight a battle against his hearing aids.

I heard some fumbling as the phone passed hands, and then my gran's delicate voice, "Hello?"

"Hi, Gran! How are you?"

"I'm good thank you, and you?"

"Yeah, I'm great!" I spoke in a slightly too high-pitched voice as if I was working in customer service.

"I was just phoning to chat!"

"Your dad tells us you're staying in England for the weekend."

"Yeah! It's boiling down here, how is the weather back at home?" It was small talk, but I was treasuring this conversation.

"Not too bad, but we've not been out much, you know? Your grandpa's knee has been quite sore again."

"Oh no, really?"

"And how is Jake?" Gran's voice rose in inflexion, suddenly changing the subject. They adored Jake, from day one. Although anyone who met Jake adored him; he was one of those easily likeable people.

"He's great! He's working tonight, thought, 4 pm to midnight." I came across as sympathetic for the long shift, but internally I was as equally grateful for his schedule as I was for Olivia's.

I heard my grandpa in the background, "When's the wedding? You've got to get engaged before I die!"

I chuckled as I heard my gran shush him. This was a joke my grandpa liked to make often, but it touched me that they were so eager to accept Jake into the family officially. Of course, the idea of my grandpa dying was horrible, but the joke alluded to our family's morbid sense of humour.

"Well, I'll let you go anyway, have a good weekend, I was just phoning to say hi," I said, as earnestly as I could, "I love you both!"

"Alright, well, love you," my gran said, ending the phone call with a small laugh.

To someone else, or rather to anyone else, that phone call was a simple conversation. A grandchild checking in on her grandparents. I didn't have the courage to admit to myself why I had made that phone call; I simply picked up my bags and made my way to the hotel.

Having only nipped in earlier to check-in, I now had the chance to fully examine the room, which was certainly a step down from the hotel I woke up to this morning. There was a single bed in the corner, versus the double-sized one I tossed and turned in at 6 am, and a small television hanging from a stand above a writing desk. The green paint that covered the walls closely resembled bile, and it created an even uglier juxtaposition with the orange carpet under my feet.

The first thing I did was shower. I felt the welcome coldness from the water run over my body, and through my hair. For the first time today, I felt clean and fresh. The sourcing weather couldn't penetrate the bathroom or take away the coolness of the water.

After stepping out of the shower, wrapping my hair into a towel and sliding into new clothes, I lay my purchases out on my bed and examined them with some interest.

Children's stationery set. Matches. Two litres of alcohol.

I opened the stationery set, tossing away the animal print ruler, the unsharpened pencil and the comically small rubber. The sharpener, however, I kept. Using the end of some scissors I found within my make-up bag, I turned the small screw in the centre of the sharpener until it gave way and the blade fell out.

I aligned the box of matches to sit next to the blade; the size difference ruined any potential symmetry in their positions.

I opened one of my litre bottles, and took a swig, grimacing as it burned the back of my throat. I put the other one in the mini-fridge underneath the desk; a cold treat for me later on.

I reached into my suitcase and pulled out my prescription medications: antidepressants and anti-seizures. That was me, Heather: the depressed epileptic.

I took a deep breath, closing my eyes and feeling the air fill my lungs to a bursting point, before letting it out through a slow exhale.

And then, I began the process of killing myself.

***

I had accepted my upcoming death with as much formality and emotion as would be present when booking a doctor's appointment, or getting a bus ticket. It wasn't something to think twice about, it was just something that had to be done. Work, lunch, shower, commit suicide.

If I considered my life, I arguably had no excuse to be depressed. I had, for all intents and purposes, a perfect existence. I wasn't lacking in anything; family, friends, education, love. And yet, the chemicals in my brain held a meeting and elected to make me miserable regardless.

That's what some people fail to realise. You get stormed with questions such as "Why?" and "What happened to cause your depression?", but that doesn't mean you can answer them. Sometimes, people are just sad.

Hopelessly, irreparably, terminally sad.

When people tell me to simply "think positivity", I just want to stare at them and say, "It feels like my mind is rotting from the inside out."

There was no one point in my life that created the darkness in my head, it simply grew over time, which people often failed to understand. For years, the negativity worsened and poisoned my life around me; demolishing my self-esteem, my motivation and my outlook for the future. This was until it got to the point where living simply didn't feel like a viable option anymore, and that the darkness of death was a lesser demon to face than the darkness in my head.

And yet, during all this time, I was not an unsuccessful person. I passed my exams, maintained work and travelled. I had meaningful, long-term friendships with many people I loved deeply, and I had a romantic relationship that felt like it was lifted straight out of a novel.

I was funny, smart, and extroverted. I would drop anything to step up and help anyone. I was the person who welcomed the newcomers and made them feel comfortable. I was uninhibited and up to do anything. I was the one who hosted parties, made plans, and brought people together.

I was a friend, a colleague, a partner, a daughter, and a person.

But all that overwhelming positivity I poured out constantly didn't weaken my depression, it simply hid it. No one ever suspects the loudest person in the room.

As I said, I could not pinpoint the exact moment in my life that it began. I had an ideal childhood. My home life was warm and peaceful and I did well in school. I didn't have lots of friends, but rather a handful of best friends, and that suited me just fine.

When I began high school, it crept up on me. Like how cold would slowly take over your body; beginning with a little fatigue and a runny nose, and ending with you in bed for a week, barely able to lift your head.

Then the self-harm began, which went from manageable to uncontrollable seemingly overnight. It was almost ingrained into my routine; come home from school, change my clothes, lock the bathroom door, hurt myself, and then do homework. Once my arms had become permanently scarred, I began to take apart my thighs, stomach, ankles and, on occasion, my breasts. I stopped wearing short sleeves, and on the occasions I did, I would wear tubular support bandages and feign arm sprains from rugby. Although everyone saw through my blatant lies; no one commented on it.

My school did get involved when the panic attacks started, but I don't think my symptoms gave them much choice. I suffered from some extreme physical distress when in my fits of anxiety; my limbs would shake and tremble until I was immobile. I would violently hyperventilate and openly weep. It was hard to disguise that part of my instability from the faculty. Consequently, I got mandatory therapy both with a school counsellor and some non-memorable psychiatrists.

The school counselling was uncomfortable at best, as it was group therapy with other people from my age group in school who faced similar anxiety issues. Opening up one-on-one was hard enough, but I was not about to do so when I had a crowd of faces watching me; especially when the said crowd was full of people, I was spending my school career with.

However, nothing compared to the misery of my experience with the psychiatrist.

I likened her to the human equivalent of a wooden plank, although saying that was somewhat an insult to planks. It would not have taken much convincing to tell me she was a robot, programmed to say only the most tone-deaf questions and statements, whilst holding absolutely no facial expressions.

I had casually mentioned that at that time I had a girlfriend, and was beginning to identify as bisexual, which was not something personally I considered an issue, nor was it greatly affecting my life. My psychiatrist concluded that the cause of my anxiety was the fact that I had not come out to my parents, and brought them into the room, conducting what felt like an involuntary outing. And, of course, my parents weren't phased at all, and simply asked to meet my then-sweetheart.

She then declared that I would not need any further sessions, and brought our time together to a grinding halt. I shook myself off the idea of therapy and counselling and vowed to keep myself to myself.

Eventually, the panic attacks became few and far between. However, that did not mean I was getting better. In fact, it was only then that my eating disorder truly came into full swing. I had swapped one coping mechanism for another. I was making my way around all the most ill-advised ways to manage problems.

For around six months, I was caught in a disgusting cycle of starving, binging and purging. I would barely eat for days, then demolish my own weight in sugary snacks, before throwing it up again. I became anaemic and malnourished,

30

looking sickly skinny, which was an unfitting look when you considered how tall I am. Eventually, I clawed my way out of that pit too and settled into a mental health pattern of crying, cutting and isolation.

By the time I reached my final year of high school, I was manic. I never attended a full day in school; continually skipping classes to avoid having to see anyone. I picked up smoking to cope; a habit I luckily dropped about a year later. I was being continually hounded by teachers for my absences, but frankly, I didn't care. I didn't offer them any explanation for my truancy, just shrugged and apologised. I was still completing my work and passing my exams, so as far as I was concerned, my physical presence during class time was unnecessary.

My friend group throughout high school was incredibly toxic, so I gained no support from them. We sat at the middle tier of popularity; not popular, but not cripplingly unpopular either. It was at that halfway point. Regardless, the people I associated with were poisonous. You were their friend one minute, then treated with a cold shoulder the next, while you tried to figure out exactly what it was you had done wrong this time. They weren't subtle with their two-faced behaviour, and when you entered a room, you knew when they had just been talking about you. The second I left school permanently, I escaped them and didn't look back.

One particularly painful moment always stuck out for me when I thought back on my school days. It happened in my third year English when I sat next to one of my friends. She had fallen out with me, for absurd reasons I cannot even recall. However, I was struggling. I was neck-deep in my pool of depression, and I was desperate to talk to her; I needed help.

She half-heartedly listened to me explaining how I was battling my mental health. After I finished my emotional speech, she turned to me and said, "Can you not mention your depression too much? Some of us have real problems to deal with."

I crawled further into my cave of hopelessness and convinced myself for a long time that my problems weren't bad enough to be real.

Overall, I was a nervous walk-over in high school. When I look back at the things I let happen to me, I pity myself.

My high-school boyfriend once broke up with me because he had feelings for another girl. I asked her out on his behalf, and when she rejected him, I got back together with him the next day. How can one person be so desperate for love?

Once, an exceedingly popular guy – I think his name was Craig? – came into school with a sling. He sat next to me in Geography and told me he was faking his injury to get out of school work. What did I do? I willingly took all his notes for him, on top of my own, so the teacher wouldn't catch on and make him do his own work. I can't even be mad at him for taking advantage of me; I was a walkover, and everyone knew.

It took being with Jake for a year to have some level of awareness of the wrongs that occurred in that relationship. It took me a while to realise that most girlfriends don't have boyfriends who think it is acceptable to turn up two and a half hours late to meet you, with no valid excuses. And most people don't apologise for being upset when they discover the same boyfriend had been sexting your best friend behind your back.

Most people realise that feeling threatened by their boyfriend is a red flag. And most boyfriends don't tell their girlfriends that their vagina looked and tasted disgusting during oral sex, and refuse to do it whilst simultaneously expecting it to be given to them. Most boyfriends don't make you want to harm yourself.

I will admit that I wasn't a saint either, and during our last few months, when we were in a period of relationship limbo as we tried to figure out whether we would stay together or break up, I slept with someone else and lied to him about it. Despite how much I resented my then-boyfriend, I felt guilt at my actions, because that wasn't the type of person I wanted to be, regardless of whatever fucked up relationship I was in.

Although I felt guilty, I didn't feel regret. Maybe that made me a worse person as a result. I don't condone cheating, but if you tally up his mistakes versus mine, I came out on top.

I had convinced myself things would be different when I went to university, to study media. I would be able to escape school, start a new chapter, and begin over. However, nothing changed. I failed to click with my fellow students, my attendance dropped, and I eventually dropped out of university altogether. My university career passed so fast, that I often forget that part of my life actually happened.

I worked part-time in a furniture store for a year, trying to figure out what the hell I was going to do with myself. I felt like a failure in every sense of the word. I had let my mental health minimise my chance of further education.

Be that as it may, I found a small beacon of hope upon discovering my current college course. It was as exclusive as it could come, only accepting around thirteen people, at most, a year. It was based in England, but with the opportunity to study at home for the majority of the time, as long as you were willing to travel to England for a couple weeks every two months or so to study collectively as a group.

Despite my near minuscule chance to be accepted, I applied, found luck on my side for once, and was following my dream, for the second time, of studying toward a career in the media.

I had sworn my mental health wouldn't sour this experience for me. And yet, I had only made it a little under a year into my studies before I found myself saying goodbye to everything that had been handed to me.

I thought about my sombre personal history as I sat, swaying slightly from the combined tipsiness, overdosing and blood loss. I was shaking, and I couldn't tell if it was from terror or intoxication, or simply both.

Depression isn't fucking poetic. It slowly trickles into your life. It starts with a few low days, some tears, and maybe some occasions bad decisions. Before you know it, you are flooded with waves of achingly negative thoughts. Sometimes you feel hopeless. Sometimes you're uncontrollably manic. Depression has a remarkable way of making you feel everything at once, and nothing at all.

It had never felt like I was living. It felt like I was killing time.

My emotions and thoughts were scattered, and just too out of reach for me to piece them together and make sense of them. I felt weakened, and an endeavour I felt so sure of committing for over a week suddenly seemed horrific.

I was a few hours into my attempt. I couldn't tell if I was regretting my choices, or I was simply scared of my worsening condition. I couldn't tell if I wanted to live, but I was beginning to want to put that outcome into the hands of someone else, like a medical team.

I was clutching my phone, leaving a fingerprint of blood on the screen. I couldn't peel apart my feelings into something clear; I just knew I ought to be seeking help.

Yet, I was still, as always, conflicted. I was *ready* to die. I had tied up my loose ends and had my final conversations with those I was able to reach out to. I had been nervous, but not due to feelings of uncertainty, it was simply due to the seriousness of what I intended to do. Up until this moment, I had no self-doubt. No second-guessing. Nothing but a complete commitment to passing away, however gory it may be.

Many suicide attempts were impulsive, but mine wasn't. At least, I didn't consider this impulsive. I had planned it meticulously for a week and even had a vague idea of what I wanted to do before I even travelled down to England.

I tried to figure out why I felt this sense of remorse, but it was like my brain had locked off certain parts of itself. It was forcing me to feel all these emotions, but it refused to tell me why. It wasn't fair. For years I had endured the emotional agony of my mental health problems, all day, every day. Like a toothache that you can't ignore; a constant dull throbbing pain, always in the background. And now, when I found a way out, and when the road signs began to point to an exit, when I was about to pull the tooth out, I couldn't completely devote myself.

Why couldn't I have faced this hesitancy before I began the whole affair? I could have binned my alcohol, my children's stationery set and my matches. I could have taken a walk, grabbed some takeout, got cosy in bed and watched some trashy, lifetime, guilty pleasure television. I could have told no one of this, and rocked up to college on Monday with my friends being none the wiser.

But now? I had to phone for help.

Who was I supposed to phone? I felt that I was unable to justify phoning 999. What if someone else needed more urgent care than me? What if I took help away from someone truly suffering? That would be a horrid level of guilt to face.

I'd have to phone NHS 24, the hotline for around-the-clock medical advice. They'd advise me what to do. I was probably fine. They'd tell me to sleep it off, and maybe force me to speak to a mental health nurse.

I wiped the blood off my phone screen, onto my shorts, and dialled. 111.

The phone rang five times before someone picked up.

"Hello, welcome to NHS 24. This phone call is being recorded for security purposes. Can I ask your name?" A woman's voice chimed through.

"Hi, yeah, it's Heather Thompson." My voice was shaky, but I felt the habitual need to speak in an overly polite tone of voice.

"And can I confirm that this is the number I can contact you on, should our phone call get disconnected for any reason?"

"Yeah, yeah, that's it."

"And can I ask, Heather, where are you phoning from?"

I gave the woman the name of the hotel, and the town I was in. I wasn't a local, I wouldn't be able to get more specific than that.

"Okay, thank you. So why have you phoned NHS 24 today?"

"I, uh, tried to kill myself."

It felt incredibly bizarre to say that aloud. I had tried to kill myself. Perhaps it was too late; perhaps I was already dying, and this phone call was meaningless. Maybe this lady would be the last person I ever spoke to.

Does it count as a failed suicide attempt if I was the one to phone for help? Or does that just mean I had given up trying to give up? I wasn't sure.

"Okay, Heather, can you tell me what you did?"

She was saying my name too much. It was probably something she had been trained to do. "Use their name to make it more personal and more comfortable!" Well, it certainly wasn't comforting me. It felt too awkward, even my friends didn't use my name that often.

"I cut over my thighs and arms. I've drank a fair amount, I'm slightly drunk. I've taken some tablets too." I felt incredibly self-conscious reiterating what I had done to this stranger.

"Alright." I heard her typing, noting down what I was saying to her. "What did you use to cut yourself with? Is there a lot of blood loss?"

"A blade from a pencil sharpener. And yes, there is a lot of blood."

More typing.

"What tablets did you take, and how many?"

"I have prescription tablets for my epilepsy and depression. I took them. I think I took about forty, but I don't know, I lost count."

Further typing.

"And you said you were drinking, how much have you had to drink?"

"About a litre and a half, give or take."

Yet more typing filled the momentary pause in the conversation.

"Are you experiencing nausea, light-headedness, vomiting, headaches and/or blue lips or skin, also known as cyanosis?"

"Yes to the nausea, light-headedness and headaches. No vomiting or blue skin."

"And you say you have epilepsy, so you're at risk of a seizure?"

"Yeah, I suppose so."

I wondered if she had a checklist in front of her, with questions she had to ask. The entire phone call felt incredibly formal.

I wasn't entirely sure what to do with myself whilst I was having the conversation, so I paced the room; leaving drops of blood behind me, like footprints. I pulled at a loose thread on my shorts and felt my chest ache with nerves. I grabbed my bottle and took another drink.

"Do you have any family history of heart problems or other similar health issues?"

"No."

"Okay, Heather, do you have a way to get to the nearest hospital as soon as possible?"

"No, I'm not local. I'm here for a college visit, I'm not even sure what the nearest hospital is," I explained my situation to her.

"In that case, I am going to have to send for an ambulance and some paramedics to pick you up."

"Wait, really?" My heart sank into my stomach.

"Yes, it's vital that you get seen to. Can you remind me of where you are right now?"

I repeated the address of the hotel, adding that I was here for college, so I couldn't be overly specific, as I wasn't particularly familiar with the area. I apologised.

"It may be a while," the woman explained, "we're incredibly busy today, and short on ambulances and staff. But they will be there, don't worry."

"No, I understand." My voice was so high-pitched it almost sounded like a squeak. "Obviously, you need to go and help others who are more serious first."

"No, you need help too, don't think like that. We'll be sending someone to you as soon as possible," the operator said sweetly, but firmly.

"Okay," I replied, meekly, "I'll phone the front desk and ask them to let the paramedics into my room when they get here."

"Thank you. If there are any changes to your circumstances, if you feel worse, for example, please do phone back, don't wait for the medical team to arrive."

"I will, thank you."

"Okay, Heather, thank you for phoning, it was the right thing to do."

I wasn't too sure I agreed with her.

"Thank you," I repeated.

The woman offered her goodbyes and then hung up. I let out an unsteady breath.

So there I was standing, in England, in a hotel room, waiting for an ambulance to take me to the hospital. No one knew. I was alone, sick, and distressed. I wasn't sure what to do with myself, but I knew I'd have to phone the hotel's front desk. It wouldn't be fair to just let an ambulance rock up, and paramedics come storming in without warning.

There was a phone next to my bed, with a note pinned to it saying "Dial 0 for reception". I picked the phone up; it felt smooth and cool in my hand. I hit the zero with my quivering finger. I didn't want to do this but I had to.

"Hello, this is reception, how can I help you?" a cheery voice, belonging to a man, answered.

"Hi, so, what it is," I began, "I'm not very well, and paramedics are being sent to the hotel to pick me up, I was just wondering if you could send them up when they get here? I'm in room three."

"Oh! Right okay. Is there anything we can do for you whilst you wait?" The receptionist sounded momentarily shocked, before returning back to his bright, customer service voice.

"No, no! I'll be fine until they get here. I just didn't want them to turn up without informing you why," I said. Classic Heather; terrified of inconveniencing anyone.

"Thank you for letting me know, please phone if you need anything, I'll send them up when they get here, I hope you feel better soon!" The words came pouring out.

"Thank you," I squeaked, before hanging up immediately. I didn't have it in me to continue with a fake and cheery conversation.

Maybe I should have said, "Hey, I tried to kill myself and I've bled all over your floor, bathroom and bed sheets. Sorry about that."

It was awfully inconvenient that my actions had consequences.

The more I considered it, the more I realised that I didn't have the strength to face this by myself. I needed someone, someone who wasn't an unfamiliar medical face that was only concerned with my vitals, or a hotel receptionist who was way in over their head.

I wanted Jake. Even if he didn't know what to do, or say, his presence made me feel safe. I needed that security with me right now. I wanted to feel the warmth of his embrace and the comfort of his voice telling me things were going to be okay. If it came from him, just maybe, I would be able to believe it.

However; I couldn't. Jake was six hundred miles away, at work. Even if I did tell him, it would only cause untold panic. He wouldn't be able to leave work and travel down to me. He would feel hopeless, stressed, and unable to help. I knew realistically I would have to tell him. But not tonight, or at least, not right now. Perhaps when I met the paramedics and had a clearer idea of my situation, I could tell him.

Even so, I needed a companion. But my options were low. Anyone back home was automatically vetoed. Olivia was at a BBQ. Ruaridh was similarly busy. I wasn't comfortable opening up to any other students with something this hard-hitting, at least, not yet. Well, except Jamie.

That could work. I already knew he wasn't doing anything tonight, and he was only a few hours away. So if I needed him in person that could be manageable. But God, what would telling him do to our friendship?

I clutched my phone staring at his name on the screen.

It just took one text and he'd know. I'd have someone to talk to as I waited for the ambulance. Someone to chip off a little bit of the crushing pressures of the situation. And texting Jamie, of all people, was most logical.

But texting him, telling him what I had done, would cross a line. I couldn't take it back if I told him, and our friendship would never be the same again.

You're stalling. I thought to myself, bluntly.

I sighed slowly and typed.

HEATHER: *Let me know when you're home and not busy. Olivia's got the BBQ and I think Ruaridh is out too, so I need to talk to you. But if you're busy it isn't a big concern.*

That was a lie, but I wasn't about to pressure someone into a conversation, regardless of my state.

About eight minutes later, my phone faintly buzzed.

JAMIE*: As in phone? Or text?*

I considered this. How could I put what I had done into a text? Plus, the minute I told him, he would phone me.

HEATHER*: Phone. No pressure. But I need you to sincerely promise you will not get in touch with Jake. At all. Or I'll never forgive you.*

I inwardly grimaced at the thought of Jake, my boyfriend. He was at work, stacking shelves all those miles away, with no clue as to what was happening.

JAMIE*: Ya ya of course. Give me 2 mins to run into this service station and have a wee. About 60% of the way home x.*

Jamie had thrown in a kiss at the end of the text; his subtle way of expressing that he knew something was wrong and was going to be nice about it, not his usual sarcastic, albeit hilarious, self.

HEATHER*: If I hang up it's because the ambulance service arrived and I need to talk to them.*

I knew that out of context, that text was going to panic Jamie, but he needed to know that I was expecting guests, so to speak.

JAMIE: *Okay, no problem at all.*

I took a drink, shuddered bitterly, wondering why I had done this on an empty stomach, and stood up, looking around at the damage I had caused to myself, and my surroundings, for the first time.

The bed sheets were sprawled across the bed, from when I had been continually standing up and down. They were white or they were partly white, for now, bloody splodges covered them. You could almost make out the outline of where I had been sitting; the shape of my thighs and legs outlined with a higher consistency of blood. The redness continued to follow me like a trail, and you could see where I had been pacing the room. It had begun to settle into the carpet, but the blood in the bathroom still looked intensely fresh against the tiles.

I took another drink, and my phone began to light up, *Jamie.*

"Hey, you okay?"

I always wondered what conversations between us sounded like to an outsider; Jamie with his somewhat smooth Kent accent, and myself with my admittedly harsher sounded Scottish voice. We were a weird pairing, that was for sure.

"Hi, um, Jamie, I—"

I lost it. There was something about hearing someone else's voice; a friend's voice, not one belonging to an emergency services phone operator. A familiar voice, unassuming but worried. It was like that stupidly familiar accent had shattered a wall, and for the first time in hours, I had begun howling. Gross, snotty, wailing that I'm sure half the hotel could hear.

"Heather, what happened?" Jamie lowered his voice; firm but tense.

I was attempting to catch my breath and tried to complete a coherent sentence.

"Heather. Tell me what happened?" he asked me a second time.

"I tried to kill myself."

A heavy, pregnant pause hung between us.

"Oh, Heather, why? Why'd you do that?"

"I don't know, I can't answer that right now," I was sobbing down the phone, "where are you?"

"Still in the gas station. I pulled over to talk to you."

I let out a hiccup and held back my tears a little before I sat back down on my stained bed.

"No, sorry, you need to get home, you still have a few hours to drive, I'm sorry, it's okay."

I always struggled with guilt. I couldn't help it. All I would be thinking about tonight, regardless of everything, was the fact I had taken up Jamie's spare time.

"Heather, listen, no, shut up. Tell me what happened," he said.

"I'm waiting for an ambulance. They said it would be an hour and a half. And I just needed to talk to someone. I can't phone anyone at home, they'd worry cause they're so far away, and Olivia is busy and so is Ruaridh, I only really have you to talk to, I'm sorry," I rambled.

"Let me make it clear; I'm glad you phoned me. Please stop apologising. What did you do?"

"I'm a bit tipsy," I admitted. I had been drinking for a few hours now. As I spoke, I ran my thumb around the top of the bottle that was sitting between my thighs, "Had about a litre and a half already." I laughed. "Guess I needed the guts to do this."

"Right," Jamie said, stoically. I took this as an encouragement to continue.

"I've cut. Very badly, there is…a lot of blood. I'm worried about paying damages to the hotel. And, I've taken some pills. I don't remember how much now."

"What pills?"

"My prescription medication, the anti-depressants and the anti-seizures," I hesitated, "so at least I know I won't be having a seizure for a few months." I laughed weakly.

I felt like I could sense Jamie smiling at the other end of the phone, in a gas station on his way home to Kent.

"You're daft," he said sweetly.

"Please go in the car and start driving. I feel so bad about you hanging about. Please don't," I begged.

"Right, fine. But I'll be putting you on speaker and I'm gonna keep talking to you, okay?"

"Sure," I whispered.

Jamie hung up. I stood up again and stretched my legs. I turned and looked at the bed I'd been sitting on. I felt bad for the hotel staff; white bed sheets covered in blood were going to be a bitch to clean. I snorted at myself; my priorities were so messed up that I was worried about bed sheets; and not the entire fucked up situation I had put myself in.

I went into the en suite and studied myself in the full-length mirror. I was wearing PJ shorts and a baggy t-shirt. I'd figured I'd owe myself a bit of comfort by wearing them.

My legs were deeply wounded. I didn't even want to attempt to count the number of cuts that were still weeping blood down my knees, my shins, and my feet. I could feel the warmth of the blood trail down them. It was a familiar sensation as self-harm clearly wasn't something new to me.

My arms were a similar story but deeper and uglier, with blood oozing down my palms and fingers. There'd be scars.

My eyes were puffy and exhausted, and I was pale.

I wandered back into the room, drank, and sat on the bed, just in time to see my phone light up again. I picked it up.

"Okay, I'm back on the road, you're on speaker." Jamie's voice was slightly more distant, echoing in his car.

"Thank you, Jamie," I said, hoping he understood how sincerely grateful I was. I took another drink; I needed it.

"Heather, are you drinking?"

"Yeah."

"Please stop, for me."

I was taken aback by how upset he sounded and put the bottle down.

By the time the paramedics had arrived, after being let into my room by a staff member of the hotel (I was unsure if it was the receptionist I had spoken to earlier), I had been talking to Jamie for over an hour. In that space of time, I had stopped crying, and did the most incredible thing; genuinely laughed, forgetting about my troubles for a brief moment.

I hung up on him mid-sentence, however, when the door opened, I heard a voice say, "Hello?" Two paramedics came in, male and female, dawning green uniforms and clutching bags.

I thought about how the situation must have looked from their point of view: me, sitting on the bed, a tear-stained face, sitting on top of blood-soaked sheets, a pool of random objects and empty bottles around me.

What a shit first impression.

"Heather, is it?" the female paramedic asked gently. I nodded.

"Okay, I'm Maureen, this is my colleague Toby," she spoke gently as if she was scared that the slightest raised voice would send me further into the wasteland of my mental health.

"Hey, thank you for coming." As always, I was polite to a default.

"Apologies for taking so long," Toby said, as he wandered the length of my room, studying the mess I'd made with such intensity you'd assume it was a crime scene.

If the bed hadn't been so gory, I'm sure Maureen would've sat down. She seemed like the kinder of the two, and I inwardly found myself likening them to a cliched '80s' detective duo, with the hardened, experienced elder and the overly enthusiastic newbie.

"Why don't you tell us what you have done?" Maureen suggested. It sounded like an optional question, but it wasn't.

As I explained the rollercoaster I had put myself through mere hours ago, Toby picked up the empty prescription boxes spread across my bed and inspected the back of them. The intensity with that Toby was examining everything was almost comical, and I'm sure if Jake had been here, we would've been laughing at it. But, of course, he wasn't here, and I was alone with the detective paramedic duo.

"Anti-seizures and antidepressants?" Toby mumbled to himself.

"Yeah," I said lowly. I watched him pick up the boxes and place them into his bag, presumably to hand over to the hospital later on.

Maureen picked up a pair of scissors I had left lying out. "Is this what you used?"

"No, I used that," and gestured vaguely toward the blade. I explained that they were merely a tool to pop the blade out of the sharpener, but she clearly wasn't listening as she slid said scissors into her bag.

"Can I have a look at your arms?" Maureen nodded toward them. Again, not an optional question.

I stuck my arms out, like a toddler demanding to be picked up by their parents. She took my wrists and turned them, so my forearm was pointing up toward the ceiling. She frowned.

"Some of these are going to need stitches," she said bluntly.

"Seriously?" I'd never had stitches before. I hadn't even considered that as a possibility; I usually just slapped some plasters on my fresh cuts until they began to heal.

"Look at this one here." Maureen pointed at one of the wider cuts. "There is fat coming out of it."

I stared; noticing it for the first time. A lump of yellow, fatty tissue was bulging out of the gaping wound. How did I miss that? Although I suppose, in a mass of cuts, I wouldn't be paying attention to one specifically. Whereas, it was Maureen's job to notice this sort of thing.

"And these ones." She pointed at three more. "They need stitches too."

"Fuck," I swore under my breath. Not out of anger, but rather, genuine shock.

"I'll cover it loosely at the moment, but it'll need to be seen at the hospital." Maureen knelt down in front of me, armed with a large rectangle of cotton dressing, and gently put it on my arm. I felt no pain, but perhaps I was numbed from the adrenaline and alcohol.

Toby continued his search throughout my room, and he picked up a bottle of alcohol, long since emptied during my endeavour to get severely intoxicated.

"It's only, like, 15%," I said, laughing shortly, "I'm a lightweight, don't need much to get me going."

No one laughed. Tough crowd.

"And how much did you drink?" Toby continued, his face stuck in a continuous expression of deep disappointment in everything.

"About a litre and a half."

He nodded and put the bottle back down. It clearly wasn't as worthy as my medication and scissors to be put into their bags.

"Okay, so we have an ambulance outside to take you to the hospital," Maureen explained.

"Cool." I'm sure that my lack of despair in my tone surprised them, but after years of dealing with the pressures of my depression, I was easily capable of pulling back and hiding how I felt.

"You might want to change beforehand because we will be walking through the lobby," Toby suggested, nodding toward my shorts.

"Oh, yeah, sure."

I stood, a wave of light-headedness washing over me. I grabbed a pair of black trousers and wandered into the bathroom. As I pulled them on, Toby attempted, poorly, to make conversation with me, telling me that the journey would be around forty minutes. I suddenly felt very bad for Maureen, being stuck with him.

. I emerged from the bathroom, pulling my sleeves down. In comparison to how I looked five minutes ago, I was a completely new person, with my wounds and blood spill hidden.

"Can you walk okay?" Maureen frowned.

"Oh, yeah, yeah," I said confidently, despite feeling a bit shaky on my feet.

"You might want to pack a bag because you're going to be there a while," Toby added.

Without responding, I began throwing stuff aimlessly into my handbag; phone, charger, purse, and hotel room key.

We left once I had slipped my shoes on, and I could feel their eyes burning into me as I locked the door to my room.

I was reminded of a conversation I had with my colleagues over lunch and inwardly chuckled, remembering their reaction when I revealed my key to them. It was attached to a separate key chain, presumably to minimise the risk of losing it. It was heavy and wooden, annoyingly incapable of being put into your pocket. To the average person, it could be described as pear-shaped.

To us, it looked like a butt plug.

We descended down the stairs, through the lobby, and past the benches at the entrance. Despite my clothes hiding the secrets on my skin, everyone stared. I couldn't blame them; I was being escorted by two paramedics, into a parked ambulance directly outside the building. They were probably watching, attempting to guess the situation with morbid curiosity. I would too if I was a bystander.

As Maureen hopped into the driver's seat, I was helped into the back of the ambulance by Toby. I had never been in one before, but it looked underwhelming exactly as you would expect. Flooded with medical equipment that meant nothing to me, a gurney covered in a blindingly blue sheet, and two fold-out chairs secured against the wall, it wasn't exactly the picture of comfort.

I decided that I couldn't justify lying down, and opted to drop onto a seat with a mild thump. Slamming the doors shut behind him, Toby joined me on the other seat, and we buckled in, shooting off to God knows where.

Maureen had chosen not to turn the sirens on, which I was grateful for. My head was pounding, and I don't think I could have handled the shrieking of an alarm for long.

"Where are you from in Scotland?" Toby asked, as he delicately pushed up my sleeve and secured an armband onto my upper arm, taking my blood pressure. I hadn't told him I was from Scotland, but it wasn't exactly hard to figure out from my accent.

"East Kilbride, near Glasgow," I answered, frowned a little as the band tightened, rapidly increasing how uncomfortable I felt.

"You're a long way from home, what brings you here?" he continued, as he squeezed the small pump attached to the contraption.

"College, only here for two weeks."

The superficial conversation continued, as Toby asked about the nature of my studies, and I replied, growing increasingly uninterested in talking to him.

"You're taking anti-seizures, so you have epilepsy, yeah?" he probed further.

"I do temporal lobe, only been diagnosed for two years. Sorta came out of nowhere." I laughed at my pathetic health. "I take absence seizures."

"Ah, so not real epilepsy then."

I paused and frowned, wondering if I had heard that right.

My seizures terrified me. From what I was told when I was initially diagnosed, absence seizures occur on both sides of the brain at once. To be very specific, I suffer from atypical absence seizures, which means I face different symptoms from usual.

It would be difficult to know when I was seizing unless you were well versed on the process of it. I stare into space, almost as if I were daydreaming. Sometimes it can affect my muscles too, so I will smack my lips, flutter my eyelids, or rub my fingers together.

To experience an absence seizure is a confusing ordeal. It begins with an overwhelming sense of Deja vu, called an *aura*. You lose all awareness of your surroundings, not noticing if someone is talking to you during your episode. If the seizure strikes when you're talking, you'll abruptly stop in the middle of your sentence as if taking a long pause.

When I immediately come out of a seizure, it will take a few minutes before I recall where I am and who I am with. Any attempts to talk are futile as what I believe to be intelligible sentences, come out as incoherent ramblings. It is upsetting, to say the least, being suddenly struck by an attack, and to get your sense of security ripped from you. And, of course, if I happen to piss myself in public too.

I was both fortunate and unfortunate when it came to my epilepsy. I was fortunate as I only experienced seizures about four times a month, which is much less than most epileptics.

However, I was diagnosed startlingly late in life, at the age of eighteen. Due to the nature of absence seizures (alongside the fact they are most common in four 14-year-olds) they are easily missable and often put down to daydreaming. I only looked into it further because, when I casually mentioned it to my dad, he urged me to speak to the doctor.

One neurologist, one MRI and one EEG later, I was slapped with the diagnosis of, *temporal lobe epilepsy*. I was given medication and told I couldn't drive unless I went twelve months without a single seizure. In a cruel twist of fate (which, at this point, I'm always expecting in my life), I was two weeks away from sitting my practical driving test. Eight months of lessons down the drain because my brain is so dysfunctional that it handed me a seizure disorder, on top of the always-present depression.

Although they typically only last 10–20 seconds, a seizure will knock me down for up to a few days afterwards. I'll feel exhausted, and weak, and if I have one seizure, I'll typically have more in the following days; like my brain is performing an encore no one asked for.

When I was diagnosed, I wasn't particularly well versed on what an absence seizure was. When I first met with my neurologist, they began listing what felt like, to me, random, unconnected events; phasing out, the sense of Deja vu, the exhaustion. Turns out that was a form of seizure.

It wasn't surprising that I didn't know much about absence seizures, it isn't particularly a represented condition in the media. Films and television shows will choose the 'sexier' seizure; the one where the character hits the floor, vomiting, shaking and successfully drawing out shock from the audience. There is nothing exciting about someone staring into space.

I wasn't one for confrontation, particularly toward strangers, so I offered a short 'Yeah' in response. Inside, however, I was nauseated with anger at his attitude.

Sorry, my seizures don't live up to your standards, I thought bitterly.

Completely against continuing the conversation, I let silence fall in the ambulance as I listened to the traffic around us, and watched the sky darken outside. I was lightheaded, which I couldn't even pretend was unexpected. I just wanted to lie down and sleep for a bit. Anything for a brief escape from the consequences of what I'd done.

"Any questions?" Toby eventually asked.

"Yeah, where exactly am I going?"

"You don't know?" He raised an eyebrow. I'm sure he was probably just surprised, but I took it as judgement. I had safely concluded that he was an asshole, so I wasn't going to change my opinion.

"Well, no, I'm not from here, I only know where my hotel and college are."

I was feeling quite light-headed; the brightness of the lights was finally getting to me.

"The nearest hospital to you is in Redditch," Toby explained, looking at his watch, "we'll be there soon."

I didn't like the vagueness of the word 'soon'. And I had no idea where Redditch was in relation to my hotel. They could've been taking me anyway, and I would be none the wiser.

I offered Toby a nod, but it wasn't a particularly convincing one. He turned his back to me and began doing whatever it was paramedics do when they're ferrying a suicidal young adult to the hospital.

I closed my eyes, trying to focus on anything but my waves of nausea, and the bouncing off the road.

I arrived in A&E approximately two hours after I phoned the paramedics, which made it around five hours since I began my self-sabotage, and made it around 8 pm in terms of time.

I at least knew that I was somewhere in Redditch, but I didn't know exactly where; I'd never actually been there before. I was in a wheelchair, sitting in the corridor clutching my bag, and speed texting Jamie, who'd finally made it home.

A&E was flooded with patients, typical for a Friday night. About five other people were sitting in wheelchairs in the corridor alongside me, and one woman was in a portable bed, looking haggard whilst clutching her stomach and moaning lowly.

After handing a nurse the items they'd picked up from my room, Toby and Maureen had said goodbye to me, patted me on the back and wished me luck. I was alone for a considerable future, despite being surrounded by so many people. I could hear one gentleman from his room, yelling out "HELLO?" over and over, every ten minutes or so, until someone came in to assist him. He sounded quite rude; I felt bad for the staff.

Jake had been and gone on his work break, and I spoke to him during it as if everything were fine. I felt sickened by my lies, but it wasn't time to tell him yet. I wasn't even sure how I could tell him something like this. I hadn't even begun to think about my parents or my other friends.

I tried to ignore the nurses rushing around me, the unmistakable sounds of vomiting, and everything else that was making me entirely too uncomfortable. It wasn't as easy to ignore how I felt physically, however. I could feel my trousers sticking to my cuts and the dried blood that had run down my foot. My stomach was churning from the pills and alcohol, and I had simply exhausted myself from the entire night.

Most of all, however, I was terrified. I was alone in a hospital so far away from home, with an unpredictable weekend ahead of me.

In my bitter hatred toward myself for not telling Jake, my thoughts drifted back to how I met him. I adored our story; it was unique and incredibly fitting for the relationship we were in.

About three years ago, Ryan had approached me, asking me to act in his student film for college. Being my childhood friend, I of course happily offered my less-than-mediocre acting services. He informed me that he had asked some of his other friends to help out; Sam, Ben, and, of course, Jake. I hadn't met any of them before and was incredibly nervous.

The movie plot was endearingly pointless and followed five friends house-sitting for a mutual friend (played by none other than Ryan himself). During that time, they face the vicious wrath of murderous balloons, which kill you upon touch. It was a storyline to rival award-winning blockbusters.

My first few scenes were alongside Ryan, as he showed my character, around his house, detailing the duties required of her in his absence. Following this, I began my scene with Sam, who I had only met about half an hour before. The scene was simple; Sam came and sat on a stool at the breakfast bar, whilst I poured him a glass of tap water and we discussed the plans for the party later.

I turned the tap on too forcefully, and the water shot everywhere, bouncing off the glass in my hand and splashing me in the face. A brief pause filled the room, before Sam and I began weeping with laughter. We have since liked to define that moment as the exact moment our friendship began.

Throughout the day, I filmed a scene with everyone. I liked them immediately, with their ridiculous sense of humour and bursting energy. Jake later told me that they had been worried I wouldn't get along with them for those exact reasons, but that, of course, could not be further from the truth.

The most vivid memory for me, bar shooting balloons with Nerf guns in the name of art, was laying my eyes on Jake for the first time. He was brilliantly red-headed, coupled with a matching, thick beard that could have made any grown man envious. He was akin to a Viking; the picture of manliness. But his gentle smile and striking blue eyes gave him the aura of approachability. I instantly felt at ease around him. Even our first conversation, where I had given him the Wi-Fi password, is a memory I wouldn't forget quickly, simply because it involved *him.*

Filming took around two months, and by the end of the process, Jake and I had begun dating, and I had become integrated into the exclusive friend group dubbed, *the Struggle.* It took meeting him a few times before either of us had the guts to text each other, but once it began, it never stopped. The conversation flowed, and eventually, he asked me to be his girlfriend on my seventeenth birthday, as we sat in what soon became our favourite Chinese restaurant.

I'm not an overly romantic person, but I couldn't deny that being with him was pure bliss. He continually impressed me with his motivation, being both a university student and an employee in a local supermarket. He was adventurous and yet would also get excited over lying in bed, eating pizza and watching movies. Simply put, we just *understood* each other.

Had I not truly believed he would be better off without the weight and pressure of supporting me and my illness, I likely wouldn't have attempted.

I kept repeating to myself that it wasn't time to tell him yet. It was a weak reassurance.

I brought myself back to the present and continued texting Jamie, giving him updates. I felt bothersome, but couldn't stop myself from flooding his inbox.

HEATHER*: I made you my emergency contact, is that okay?*

JAMIE: *Course it is.*

HEATHER: *They're worried because they don't know what my anti-seizures can do to me during an OD. Talking about keeping me overnight. I'll need to phone the hotel and talk about the blood and ask them to clean it. If they let me out tomorrow I don't know how I'm getting to the hotel again.*

When I had arrived, and the paramedics explained to the nursing staff what I had used to overdose with, they were frankly stunned. Then I was informed that whilst using antidepressants is very common during a suicide attempt; using anti-seizures was a new one, and they weren't sure what was going to happen to my body.

JAMIE: *That's a good plan, staying the night is probably wise. I'd imagine the hotel might have checked your room? But good to be in contact. If you're comfortable with Olivia knowing, she isn't far and could give you a lift?*

HEATHER: *Can you tell Olivia? I can't face it.*

JAMIE: *I'll tell her in a bit, I'll see what she's doing. Just relax yourself, I can leave it until tomorrow if you don't want to be bothered by her?*

HEATHER: *I don't want to annoy her. She said she wouldn't be at the BBQ long but I don't know. Don't want to be selfish and pull people away.*

I paused, then sent a second message.

HEATHER: *I cannot express my gratitude to you. You're an amazing friend, I'm glad I phoned you.*

I watched the three dots pop up on the screen; an indication Jamie was typing. I looked around the hallway. One of the wheelchair-bound people who were with me in the corridor had gone, which was promising as it meant people were being attended to.

JAMIE: *Okay, if she is not busy I'll let her know. And don't mention it, I needed some more to put on my CV before I apply for a job in therapy.*

I giggled at Jamie's response. He knew me and my humour well.

HEATHER: *You should be in therapy, man! I was having tablets every five minutes and cutting non-stop until we spoke. Honestly though, thank you and I love you. If Jake knew what you were doing right now, he'd be so grateful too.*

I heard someone throwing up again; the depressing chorus of the A&E waiting room.

JAMIE: *Love you too, mate, glad I could be there and so glad you reached out. You did fantastically.*

I nearly began crying again at Jamie's response. Before tonight, I liked to believe that he and I were close; but maybe not in the traditional sense of a friendship. We spoke every day, but to tease each other and make jokes; nothing too heavy of a topic. I suspected after tonight, we'd never fall back into just being like that again – how could we? We were going through too much now.

I began replying to Jamie when I felt a horrendous churning in my stomach. Before I could react appropriately, I leaned over the side of my wheelchair and vomited onto the floor, my throat burning.

I heard a few gasps from disgusted onlookers and the sound of footsteps hurriedly coming over as a nurse appeared.

"I am so sorry, that is so embarrassing," I wheezed, suddenly out of breath, as my eyes began tearing up. I was feeling cripplingly overwhelmed.

I had extreme emetophobia, that is, a phobia of vomit. Likely a consequence of my previous bulimia, I could barely handle it. And that extended across all areas of throwing up; watching people be sick, smelling sick, seeing sick, hearing people be sick, and of course, physically being sick. Even hearing or using the word 'vomit' sent chills down my back. So, my mild anxiety attack was not atypical, however, it was frustrating.

"Don't be silly! Are you okay? Can I get you some water?" The nurse fussed over me as she cleaned up my mess. I thanked her and accepted the water eagerly when she returned with it, using it to desperately drown the taste of bile in my mouth.

I gave Jamie my less than pleasant update.

HEATHER: *Guess who puked? Me. God, I'm burning up. It was in the corridor too, I'm properly embarrassed. Nearly started crying.*

JAMIE: *I bet you did! Not surprised. But shit happens, it's a hospital. Don't worry about the OD coming back up, it'll help you in the end that stuff can't stay in your stomach.*

Jamie was incredibly considerate, and I could tell how hard he was trying, which brought back up my deep-seated feelings of guilt at pulling him into this mess.

HEATHER: *God, I wish you were here. I'm a vomity, bleeding, crying mess. As per usual, of course.*

JAMIE: *If you want me to tell Olivia, she might be able to come.*

I'd have loved nothing more than for Olivia to be there. She was kind to a fault and so comforting, but I didn't want to pull her from her Friday night to deal with this awfulness. I had already ruined one person's weekend, I should be taking a break before I ruin another. And yet, all I wanted was to be able to speak to her.

I couldn't help but feel selfish yet again; torn between wanting to avoid any more feelings of guilt, but desperately wanting support whilst I trembled, alone, in this hospital corridor. I told myself, that if the tables were turned, I would want to know regardless of what activity I was currently caught up in, so Olivia would likely want to know too.

HEATHER: *Actually, yes, could you speak to her? I honestly think you saved my life tonight, Jamie. I can never repay you.*

I figured he would be getting bored of my constant thanks, but it felt like I'd never be able to express the gratitude I felt toward him.

JAMIE: *Of course. And, you saved your life by reaching out. All I did was talk to you.*

I wondered what he would say to her. Would he phone her? Text her? Knowing Jamie, I would guess that he would phone. In the meantime, I just sat like a spare part in my unnecessary wheelchair.

Just then, a nurse approached me; the same lady who had the pleasure of cleaning up my vomit moments ago.

"Heather? We're going to take you into a treatment room to get your stitches in." She smiled at me. I offered a nod in return. Toby and Maureen must have told the A&E team about my deeper cuts.

She wheeled me down the hall, and I was suddenly self-conscious about my weight, hoping that she wasn't having too much hassle pushing me about. My thoughts and concerns were bouncing all over the place.

"How's your stomach?" she asked.

"Better, yeah, still feel a bit nauseous though."

"That'll clear up soon, don't worry."

She stopped me in front of a small A&E treatment area, opened the door, and wheeled me back into the room.

"I feel a bit ridiculous being in this chair," I admitted.

"Most people do," she said sympathetically, "unfortunately, it's hospital policy for anyone who came in an ambulance, but you can pop up onto this bed for me now anyway."

I stood, my legs feeling wobbly under me, while my head was mildly spinning. I put my bag behind me on the wheelchair, and clambered up onto the bed; my legs dangling off the side.

It was one of those hospital beds that got completely cleaned after every patient. It had a white spread over it, which was uncomfortably similar to plastic sheeting you'd cover your couch with when painting the living room walls. I could hear it crinkle under me whenever I moved.

The room overall was rather minimal, with a strong smell of cleaning chemicals filling the air. There was a blood pressure monitor to my right, and a sharps bin to my left at the end of the bed. There was a sink, with a huge poster above it, screaming at you about the importance of washing your hands. A couple chairs were pushed against the wall, similarly covered in awkward plastic linen, like the bed. A few wooden shelves completed the room. It was deeply impersonal and quite intimidating as a result.

The nurse momentarily left the room, before coming back, pushing a small, metal table with an array of equipment sitting on the top. It didn't take much deduction to realise that said tools were intended for me.

"Let's see your arm," she said, whilst pulling some rubber gloves on. I pushed up my sleeves delicately.

I had not had the chance to fully examine the deeper wounds on my arm. When I had been in the hotel, attempting, I was too caught up in the overall situation. And with the blood spillage over my arms, I wasn't able to see too much of what lay underneath; the actual cause of the blood. If I had been too immersed in making phone calls and drinking to notice this glaringly obvious trauma, what other significant bodily harm could I have potentially overlooked?

So when the nurse, who had yet to tell me her name, slowly peeled off my dressing from earlier that night and dabbed at my open gashes with alcohol-soaked pads, I scrutinised my forearm.

My right arm looked disgusting, to put it quite frankly. Perhaps disgusting didn't even cover it. Gruesome, shocking, vile, horrific; pick your favourite. Nonetheless, I could not stop staring at it, with morbid curiosity. Much akin to a car crash.

The four cuts that were going to require stitches were diagonally patterned across my wrist; angry and red, with dried blood around the edges and the yellow, pulsing fat sticking out. In between those uglier lacerations were small, more superficial cuts. They continued up my forearm until the crook of my elbow, and whilst they weren't deep, they were numerous. My left arm was very similar, minus the need for stitches. Both arms were so reddened with drying blood that it was hard to see the paleness of my skin underneath. Although I couldn't see it presently, I knew a blanket of older, faded scars from years gone by lay under the layer of fresh injuries.

"Have you had stitches before?" The nurse's voice caused my head to snap up, coming out of my inner monologue and back into reality.

"No, I'm a bit nervous."

"Don't worry, the only part that is a bit nippy is getting local anaesthetic, and after that, it's over very quickly."

I wasn't sure I could trust that. I mean, aren't they supposed to make it seem less than it actually is, to put you at ease?

I watched her raise a syringe, examine it, and then turn to me.

"Okay, so I'm going to numb your arm now, it'll take a few injections, then we will leave it for a couple minutes to kick in."

I nodded again, like a bobblehead. I turned away, not particularly keen on watching a needle entering my flesh. It was rather ironic; self-inflicted pain was no problem, but if someone else is administering the pain, I have next to no tolerance.

I watched the window on the door, seeing staff members darting past. They certainly were busy tonight.

"I'm just going to insert the needle now," the nurse's running commentary continued.

The pain smarted for a brief second but otherwise felt bearable. I couldn't help but compare the situation to an A&E visit I had with Jake and Ben a year or so ago. That time, however, it was Ben getting stitches.

It was around 1 am, and we were walking back from the pub. Somewhere between singing at the top of our lungs, and laughing uncontrollably at nothing, Ben had managed to fall down a hill. When he rose, he was covered in mud, and we all drunkenly howled with laughter. However, upon approaching him, I noticed a sizable slit on his palm that was bleeding considerably down his wrist. He had caught it on some broken glass on his untimely descent down the hill.

"Ben, that definitely needs stitches," I had told him, mustering up all the level-headed soberness I could.

Ben had snorted at that, and said, "I've got this, don't worry."

He proceeded to turn around, and stick his injured hand in the mud, declaring that it was now clean.

"Yeah, now we definitely need to take you to fucking A&E to get that cleaned." Jake agreed with me.

So we wrapped my cardigan around Ben's hand, and jumped in a taxi to the hospital, with the driver threatening damage charges if so much as a drop of blood was spilt in his car.

If you've ever been to A&E, you'll understand that there is always a loud, drunk person or persons that are making everyone else uncomfortable. Jake, Ben and I were those people that night.

It was 3 am before we got taken into a treatment room. Jake had collapsed onto a chair in the corner, Ben lay down on the bed, and I stood. I was feeling significantly more competent by then and was certainly more put together than my two companions.

As Ben had fallen, the nurse had to rule out a concussion, or more serious head injury. She asked Ben to say the months of the year backwards, and in his drunken state, he just stared at the nurse and told her he didn't know.

With that, the nurse laughed and asked if he could at least try saying them in order. By the time he got to August, Ben was struggling and sat there saying, "I know this, I promise", over and over.

I began whispering, "September, it's September", to him, but he waved me off and drunkenly proclaimed that he didn't need my help.

Eventually, the nurse gave up and decided that he was fine, just a twat.

When it came to actually getting stitches, Ben was terrified. I assumed it was down to the alcohol because typically he was stoic and not one to easily express fear. So I held his hand and distracted him, whilst the nurse gave him five-or-so stitches.

By that point, Jake was green. He couldn't even look up, he felt too nauseated by the process. It was, admittedly, hilarious.

I wondered how Jake would have handled watching me get stitches right now, in an arguably much gorier situation. He'd have probably passed out.

A few minutes passed, and my arm felt completely numb. It was a peculiar, but not unwelcome sensation, as it had also taken away the feeling of pain from that area. Despite that, I opted not to watch a needle and thread get passed through my skin. Some things I was willing to leave to the imagination.

I just watched the ticking of the second hand on the clock above the door frame and tried to imagine what Jamie was telling Olivia at this moment.

"Right, I just want to put one more in this one, and that's you done."

A slow minute passed. I counted down the seconds on the clock, one by one.

"That's you, all finished," the nurse said triumphantly.

I glanced down at my arm. It certainly looked a sight better, considering. She had wiped all the blood away, and bar a fresh drop here or there, it looked clean. I could see the copious amount of cuts on my right arm clearly.

I had fourteen stitches across four cuts. Around each tiny entry point that the black medical thread passed through, there was a small circle of redness. My arm had already begun to bruise, with shades of purple and green beginning to creep around the closed wounds. I knew I was looking at my own arm but it didn't feel like mine. I couldn't help but wonder if this was what an out-of-body experience felt like.

"Before you go back to the waiting area, I just want to clean your other arm and put some butterfly stitches on it."

I turned my head to inspect my left arm. It was still violently bloodied and made my right arm look even better by comparison.

"What are butterfly stitches?" I asked as I watched her wipe my skin.

The nurse turned, grabbed something off her cart, and handed it to me. It was a narrow strip, which I assumed was some sort of an adhesive.

"It closes together smaller cuts, that don't necessarily need stitches, but still need a bit of help to pull the edges back together," she explained, before smiling, "no more injections needed, it's a bit like a plaster."

"That's not too bad then."

I watched her stick them down, calculating how many she was using. All in all, it was eighteen.

My arms were unquestionably a sight for sore eyes. They were clean, yes, but the spectacle of fourteen stitches and eighteen butterfly stitches was certainly ugly.

"You'll get bandaged up soon, but I want to let your arms breathe a bit first because the pressure from the dressing will hurt."

Great, I thought, *that's something to look forward to.*

By the time the nameless nurse wheeled me back to my designated area in the hallway, about twenty minutes had passed. I felt my phone vibrate in my pocket as I locked the wheels of my chair, preparing for another long wait. I saw a notification from Olivia on my screen. The message was simple and sweet, and I could tell was probably holding back a wave of emotion.

OLIVIA: *I'm here. If you need me, I can be with you.*

My thumbs bounced furiously as I typed back, trying to find the simplest way to say the one million things I wanted to say to her.

HEATHER: *I'm so sorry. I'd ask you to come but it is late and I'm just so, so, sorry.*

Apologising seemed to be my new favourite thing to do.

OLIVIA: *Don't apologise. You have no reason to apologise.*

I didn't fully believe her.

HEATHER: *I'm pretty scared. And in a lot of pain. And the staff here don't know anything about me because I'm registered in Scotland.*

This, I thought to myself, was good and bad. It was bad in regards to the fact that they had no access to any of my medical history, but they also did not have any of my family contact details. They couldn't get in touch with my parents until I provided details. I still had some power left, despite being in a wholly powerless situation. I wasn't about to tell Olivia that, however.

OLIVIA: *It's okay, I promise. You'll be okay, they'll take care of you. Are you in a room for yourself?*

HEATHER: *No, in an A&E corridor. A doctor is going to bandage my arms at some point but I've had to get stitches. They won't be able to bandage my thighs. I feel really faint like I'm going to pass out. I've already thrown up. What has Jamie specifically told you? I don't know how much you know. And sorry for not getting in touch sooner. I didn't want to ruin your BBQ.*

I was hesitant to over share if Olivia didn't want to hear the details, or if Jamie had already caught her up to speed.

OLIVIA: Okay, well let the doctors do whatever they need to do. Jamie just told me what had happened and where you are. And I didn't go to the BBQ, in the end. Don't apologise.

I felt a little bit of weight being lifted learning that I hadn't spoiled a night of various cooked meats. BBQs were actually something the Struggle and I enjoyed quite often when I thought about it.

Our go-to area was in a local country park. For a small town like ours, which was famous only for having a lot of roundabouts, you wouldn't have expected a little slice of picturesque tranquillity to be hidden away here. And yet it was and it was heavenly.

The park opened up with a zoo; pocket-sized compared to the likes of London or Edinburgh. That didn't take away from its appeal, especially when you could find the likes of meerkats and guinea pigs in such close proximity to each other. It was somewhat comical if truth be told. The zoo even offered an indoor, more tropical area, full of terrariums, with the likes of snakes and lizards in them. Although the heat from that section was somewhat stifling.

Once passing through the gates to the zoo, you could find yourself atop the beginning of a hill. And for me, personally, this was when the real adventurous part began. If you stood and gathered in your surroundings before heading downhill, you could see for miles. The forests to the right, the cars driving into the car park on the left, and the monstrously huge children's play area. You could even begin to make out the houses and flats in the distance.

If you trailed off into the forest, like we often did, you could keep yourself busy for hours. It began with a waterfall, crashing down in a mid-sized river, with a charming wood bridge offering access across.

During the summer months, you'd find people waddling about in their bare feet, alongside dogs, exhilarated, running about in the water wildly. If you continue onto the rocky footpath, created after years of being worn down by curious members of the public, you'd lead off, deep into the forest.

It was stunning; with every possible shade of green, orange and yellow. It came with a comforting lack of city noise; no cars, or buzz of people talking, just simple bird calls, the low blowing of a light breeze, and the noise of twigs snapping under you. Trees stood tall, having been growing there for longer than anyone could remember, and the seclusion made you feel tucked away from all the problems that waited for you outside the park.

Eventually, the pathway would lead to a marshland. There were wooden walkways to help you cross, and the whole area looked somewhat menacing, with the dark-coloured ooze, and the robust foliage growing out of it. Whenever I passed through, I was internally terrified that I'd fall off the platform into the mud and sink away, never to be seen again. Which, in retrospect, was an ironic fear, considering the situation I had currently put myself in.

Finally, you'd find yourself on some country back roads that if followed for about an hour or so, would actually lead you to the street I lived in. That in itself was a pleasant walk; with fields, farms, and stand-alone cottages filling your view as you meandered past.

However, it wasn't any of these areas where our BBQ was hosted at. Rather, the assigned BBQ area was at the base of the hills, sitting in between the outskirts of the forest and the children's play area. The perfect bubble between the busy and the calm.

It took me a moment of thinking before I remembered who had been there, but I smiled to myself when I remembered. There had been six of us; Jake, Gaby, Ben, Ryan, Sam and I.

It was a beautiful sunny day, which was atypical for Scotland. We all donned our own pair of sunglasses, shorts, and loose tops, hoping to get a bit of mercy from the pounding sunlight. We set up two disposable BBQs; one for me, the vegetarian, and one for everyone else. Although, I always made a point of cooking all my food quickly, so that the overwhelming majority of meat-eaters could use both grills.

I recalled taking a group photo, all of us sitting on a splintering fence that was barely keeping together, faces red from the sun, but beaming with joy. I had printed it out and hung it on my wall.

There was nothing particularly unusual about that day that stood out, that made me reflect upon it so immediately when Olivia's similar plans were mentioned. It was quite simply one of those beautiful summer days, where all you did was laugh with your friends, and exist within that moment. It was a pleasant thought to break through the bleakness of my current environment, and the momentary lapse in my attention span gave me a second to remember one of my better days.

I blinked back into reality and quickly replied to Olivia again.

HEATHER: *I'm definitely being kept in. So, if possible, it would be cool if you could visit tomorrow. Not if it is going to inconvenience you, though, of course.*

OLIVIA: *We'll arrange something. Maybe Ruaridh and I? If you're okay with telling him. Just so you aren't alone.*

HEATHER: *I don't deserve you and Jamie.*

OLIVIA: *You deserve the world.*

I doubted that very much.

Saturday

Jamie had finally gone to bed, under the stern condition that I sent him regular updates to read when he woke up, and that I would phone if things worsened. I had agreed, merely because I just wanted my friend to rest. He deserved it more than I did. Olivia had also apologised for going to sleep, but I truly didn't mind. Even ten minutes of support was ten minutes more than I felt I had earned at this moment.

I spent my time carefully detailing my updates for Jamie.

HEATHER: 1.56 am: *The doctor came in for blood tests. Got blood tests to see if my liver and kidneys have been infected. I'm getting progressively worse stomach cramps but the nausea has gone down. I'm shaking really badly, and I'm quite faint, so they've put this cannula in my arm to give me fluids, hopefully, it helps. They're going to bandage my arms too.*

HEATHER: 2.51 am: *I'm gonna be admitted into the hospital overnight and the medical team will meet me in the morning. Only took seven hours.*

It was about 3 am before I was admitted into a hospital ward out with A&E. When I got to my bed in the top left corner of the room, I pulled the curtain entirely around, and lay in bed breathing deeply for a few seconds. I knew I wouldn't sleep tonight, and it was too late to start asking questions to the nursing staff; I didn't want to wake the other patients.

I had an IV in my right arm, which made it ultimately very uncomfortable to bend or move. I also had two hospital gowns on; one worn normally, the other like a cape, as the first gown couldn't tie properly at the back. I was an incredibly depressed superhero.

The ward was as silent as it could be, considering. Monitors were beeping, nurses popped in and out for check-ups, and there was some faint snoring from another bed. I decided to just put my headphones in, listen to music, and power through until the morning; when I'd eventually have to start telling others.

Until then, the rest of my early morning was broken down into updates for Jamie.

HEATHER: 3.32 am: *Doctor said I'm showing a lot of symptoms that are worrying, stomach cramps, shaking and my pupils are huge, kinda like I'm high. I'm being monitored for 4 hours, and getting my heart tested at some point. I'll also be given more fluids.*

HEATHER: 4.58 am: *Finally got bandages. Only took, like, eight hours.*

The ward began to wake up around 6 am, allowing me to examine my surroundings properly for the first time. It was your typical six-bed ward, and I was clearly the youngest in the room by about forty years.

My contact lenses had long since dried out, and I had stupidly left my glasses in my hotel room, so I had to squint furiously to make anything out, but even then I could tell that most of the people in the room were old enough to be one foot in the grave.

It was a medical assessment unit; a place with constant surveillance for patients needing regular monitoring and diagnosis.

I felt inwardly quite lucky with my bed. I was in my own corner of the room; with the fire door next to me, so I could stare out of it at the hospital garden, even with my curtains pulled around. The sunlight was picking up, and the gentle noise of a light drizzle filled the room. It was a peaceful calm, conflicting greatly with the rest of the room.

The ceiling lights suddenly flickered on, and the day officially began.

A nurse pulled back the curtains and came over to the edge of my bed. She smiled warmly, and introduced herself as Beth, before telling me she needed to swap my IV drip.

"Hey." I greeted her, as pleasantly as I could. "No worries."

Beth stopped and stared at me wide-eyed. "I was *not* expecting that accent to come out of you."

I laughed, a genuine laugh, at the look of amused surprise on her face at my sudden Scottish accent.

Beth asked me the usual questions, "How are you?", "Do you need anything?" as she changed my IV, and confirmed that a doctor would be around to see me later on, in order to explain everything to me. She couldn't give me a rough time estimate, but that was okay. It wasn't like I had anywhere to go, I'm sure I'd be able to fit it into my busy schedule of disappointing and worrying everyone I loved.

A male nurse joined her side, asking some medical questions I couldn't translate into simple English. He offered me a polite hello and raised his eyebrows at my accent when I returned the greetings.

"I was not expecting a Scottish accent," he said.

"I was just saying that!" Beth exclaimed.

I laughed politely as Beth and her colleague began attempting to imitate my accent. I was used to this, to be honest. Working with mainly English people meant my Scottishness was somewhat comical to them, and the slight difference in my pronunciation of words, or any local slang I threw into a sentence, was something they always pointed out. I didn't understand the appeal, but then, I suppose I was used to it. Whereas, to the staff of this very English hospital, I was somewhat of a novelty.

Before Beth wandered off, she asked if I wanted any food in the meantime. I didn't, I was still cripplingly nauseous, and running on a still present drug and alcohol high. I didn't particularly fancy throwing up yet again.

And with that, I was lying there. It was too early for anyone to really be awake, and I wasn't going to hound Jamie into waking up and keeping me company. As far as I was concerned, I couldn't ask him for anything ever again.

It felt like one of those television shows where the main character is standing still, with their voiceover narrating the drama of the episodes, whilst everything around them was sped-up; a blur, merely passing by the titular character. I was lying in bed, in a ward, away from home, and life had stood still. Nothing would ever be the same for me, and this weekend was feeling like a giant, pregnant pause. Yet, all the staff around me keep buzzing around. Their day wouldn't stop, and nothing had changed for them in the past 24 hours.

I was, simply, the 20-year-old in the corner of the room who had tried to kill herself.

That's why, when a doctor threw back my curtains some hours later, it only felt like moments for me, and I had to blink furiously in confusion and look at my phone screen for reassurance of the time. *9.41 am.*

Time flies when you're having fun. But what fun was I having, exactly?

All I had been doing was sitting and twiddling my thumbs, waiting for someone (mainly Jamie) to wake up. I couldn't, or more accurately, I wouldn't watch the small portable television that hung above my bed as you had to pay to use it. Out of my petty, cheap spite, I refused to spend money on it when I could easily use my phone.

The doctor pulled back the curtains and offered a smile at me. It was a weak, half-hearted smile, and was frankly a little unnerving. It seemed incredibly fake like he was taught it during a PowerPoint presentation at his latest leadership seminar.

"Hello, Heather, I'm Doctor Thorne." He reached his hand out to me, and I took it, shaking it weakly. My IV drip flailed as my arm moved.

Thorne, I thought, *no wonder you seem like a prick.* I internally applauded myself at that pun, wishing Ethan could have been there to hear it. He appreciated a good joke. Or rather, he appreciated an awful pun. Same difference.

"So, I'm here to talk to you about what our game plan is going to be over the day, and you give you a rough idea of what to expect."

"Yeah, that'd be great, thank you."

He stood at the end of my bed, looking rigid in his brown shirt and faintly lighter brown, pressed trousers, with his glasses falling slightly down his nose. His eyes continually glanced downward at his clipboard as if it contained a script for our conversation and he had forgotten his lines.

"So, let's begin with how you're feeling, tell me about that." He stared at me expectantly.

I considered this. How did I feel? Exhausted, due to lack of sleep. Embarrassed, due to giving in and phoning for help. Terrified, due to the impending reactions of friends and family when I have to tell them.

But I had a rough idea that Doctor Thorne was looking for physical symptoms at the moment, which I was happy to give if it meant getting something to ease the situation.

"To be honest, my stomach is still cramping quite a lot. I'm really nauseous too, feeling quite weak and shaky," I explained as the doctor nodded.

"Okay, well, a nurse will be coming around within the hour to hook you up with a twenty-four-hour heart monitor. It'll just be like some small stickers being put on your chest, and it'll be attached to a small machine, it won't get in the way, but you'll need to keep it on the whole time, even if you go to the bathroom," he clarified. "It's just because of the amount of medication you took, alongside what type of medications, that we want to pay keen attention to your bodies responses."

"Does this mean I'm in all weekend? If it's twenty-four hours?"

"Yes it does, is that okay?"

I nodded. It wasn't like I had somewhere else to be. You don't typically make a lot of plans for the future when you had intended on dying the previous night.

"We'll discuss arrangements for your departure tomorrow, and we shall send a therapist to sit down and talk with you at some point before you leave tomorrow as well."

I nodded again. "Okay, yeah."

"We'll also be getting the results of your blood tests at some point, so we'll talk to you about that afterwards. Also, you'll be getting about ten bags of fluids."

My head was spinning with all this information, and yet, when Doctor Thorne asked if I had any questions before he left, I shook my head. He leaned over, and patted me on the back robotically, then darted off.

I didn't have the space between my ears to fill with more medical news. All I needed to know was that I was being tested to see if my body is still functioning okay, and I'll be updated. I needed to keep things short and sweet like this right now.

About ten minutes after Doctor Thorne thundered off, Beth came fluttering back in. Her face was lit up as if she had just been told the greatest news, and it was mildly infectious, as I found myself picking up a little during our conversations.

Beth explained that she was here to give me my anti-seizure medication, attach my heart monitor and change my drip. The whole nine yards.

I watched her take a key and unlock the small, wooden bedside cabinet next to me. I was shocked to watch her take out my prescription medication that the paramedics had confiscated the previous night. They must've been put in there just before I was wheeled in. She popped out one, and handed it to me, with a small plastic cup of water.

As I swallowed, Beth explained, "We're only giving you the necessary seizure medication right now. We've paused the rest of it until your test results come back. Don't want to risk it."

I nodded. "Makes sense."

"Okay, so for the heart monitor, I'm going to need to ask you to pop your gown down to your stomach for me. Are you comfortable doing that?" she asked kindly. I nodded again, feeling like a bobblehead.

She began preparing whatever it was she was about to use whilst I sat up, wincing as my cannula pulled at my skin. I pulled off the gown I was wearing to cover my front, feeling a slight chill on my bare chest. It wasn't unwelcome; my face had been burning up for quite some time, and I appreciated the coolness.

Lying back down, I watched what Beth was doing. She noted my staring eyes and took a second to show me what was about to be attached to me. The monitor was portable and smaller than I expected. It looked somewhat akin to a thick mobile phone, with a lanyard attached to the top, for it to hang off my neck.

Coming off it were eight wires, white and thin, like a malnourished octopus. Ending each of the wires was a small, blue sticker, which I assumed was what would be going onto me.

"You're lucky," Beth joked, "if you were a guy, I'd have to shave your chest."

I laughed. "I think that makes you luckier than me."

Beth agreed. She began placing the stickers one on each collarbone, one just above each of my breasts, one of each on my ribs, and the final two on my sternum. As she did so, she raved over my chest tattoo.

I looked down at it as she told me how minimalist and pretty it was, and I had to admit, I agreed. I had a thistle dead centre on my chest. It was small, only about three centimetres long, and it was certainly minimal, as it was a piece of black line work. I got it about two years ago, as my third tattoo.

She proceeded to ask me if my piercings hurt; drawing attention to the fact I had my nipples pierced too, currently dawning gold bars. I admitted that they had been some of my more painful body modifications, but were two of my favourites, and were completely worth it.

In total, I had seven tattoos. My first ever one, a red balloon on my left rib, was a loose reference to how I met Jake and my current friends. A balloon, just like the ones we shot with Nerf guns, in Ryan's house.

My second one was under my left, a little off-centre to the right. It was an American traditional style shark; my favourite animal. A short time after this one was when I got my thistle.

My fourth tattoo was a Ferris wheel, on my left leg, upper thigh, on the outside. It was a minimalist design. As much as I wish I could place meaning to it, I can't, it's simply a beautiful design that I fell in love with. A piece of artwork I wanted to carry with me forever. I've always maintained that a tattoo doesn't always need to have meaning, if you love a design enough to willingly get it on your body forever, then that is reason enough.

My fifth one was one I got whilst on holiday with the Struggle last year. They kept me company whilst I got a plague doctor mask tattoo just underneath my left knee, an off-centre to the right, so it was aligned with my shark tattoo. It was inevitable that I was going to get a horror-themed tattoo one day. For as long as I can remember, my dad and I have held an intense admiration for horror movies. In fact, I think an appreciation of horror was something he drilled into our family from day one after his first date with my mum was to see, *Henry: Portrait of a Serial Killer*. It never matters what kind, be it foreign, obscure, a classic or an awful modern flick, we watch them all. My mask was a comment on that, and an allusion to my relationship with my dad.

My sixth tattoo equally holds a great significance to me. On the centre of my left thigh, is a simple, yet beautiful, tattoo of Frida Kahlo. Or rather, more specifically, a flower crown with her ever famous monobrow underneath; nothing more. Frida Kahlo, alongside being an extraordinary artist, is the kind of woman I look up to. She was a fierce, bisexual feminist. But even more than that, despite being affected by continual, long-term illnesses, she chose to find beauty in her pain, through her often-experimental paintings. That's an outlook I could certainly do with adopting.

Finally, just above my left ankle, I have a small tattoo of a burning matchstick. Again, it held no personal significance to me. Or maybe it did now, as I was feeling burnt out.

Despite hurting my wrists and thighs; I had taken care to avoid my permanent artwork. Even when facing death, I did not want to leave blemishes on the parts of myself that I genuinely liked. It was depressingly funny that the fragments of myself I liked, I had to spend significant amounts of money to gain. I suppose it was somewhat akin to plastic surgery.

Whilst my tattoos were easily hidden, you only had to look at my face to see that I was pierced. My nipples, and the belly button piercing I got when I was seventeen, are certainly kept private from the public. However, my septum, tongue and nostril piercing were not as easily tucked away.

"I wish I had the courage to get mine pierced," Beth lamented, referring to my nipples. "Right, that's you done; you can put your gown back on. You don't need to do anything else with the monitor, just be careful not to knock any of the wires off. Let us know if you do, okay?"

"Okay, seems easy enough." I pulled my gown back on, flinching again as my arm ached in protest. The monitor felt heavy on my neck, but not uncomfortably so.

"Right, now I just need to change your IV and that's us," Beth declared triumphantly. She looked down at my arm. "I think it's blocked."

Gazing down, I noticed for the first time some blood pooling into the tubing of the drip. Well fuck.

"Not to worry, just means I'll need to put one into your other arm."

It wasn't until Beth had inserted a new cannula into my left arm, hooked me up, and left, that I noticed she hadn't removed the cannula in my right arm. I could bend my arms, but it was far from a pleasant sensation, so I found myself lying on the bed like a corpse, arms outstretched, and waiting for an autopsy.

How ironic.

I was in a great amount of physical distress. The secondary robe I was wearing like a cape was sticking to my back and under my arms. My arms were pulsing with pain, under the pressure of tight bandages. The inner bends of my

84

arms ached from being continually stabbed with needles. My eyes were dry, and I felt a dull throbbing behind them, which I marked up to the fact that I had neither contacts nor glasses and was persistently straining to see. I was thoroughly fatigued; physically and mentally, and where the day had barely begun for the other patients, to me, it felt like the night was never-ending.

My skin was on fire; I felt like I was back on the rooftop I sat on yesterday afternoon, feeling the unforgiving heat of the late-summer English sun directly onto my face. I was certainly experiencing some form of alcohol and drug come down from last night, and my body was feeling exceedingly worse; protesting what I had done.

Another ten minutes passed before Beth reappeared yet again, this time armed with a jug of water and a plastic cup.

"Thank you so much, I'm burning up so badly right now." I placed the back of my hand against my forehead as I spoke as if to confirm to myself that I was, indeed, still very warm.

"Let me see what else I can do about that," Beth said thoughtfully, disappearing again before I could say anything.

By the time I had poured a glass and tasted the coolness of the water against my lips, she had reappeared, table fan in tow. She plugged it in, turned it on, and almost instantaneously the air filled with a crisp chill. I relaxed into my bed, twisting my neck so I could feel the air against my face.

"Thank you, that's amazing." I sighed contentedly, feeling marginally better.

"Don't worry, I stole it from a coma patient." Beth winked at me, but I wasn't completely convinced she was joking.

"Beth," I said hesitantly, "if I tell my parents what is going on, would they be able to phone the hospital and speak to someone who can talk to them? I think they'll want to."

"I'll tell you what." Beth looked at me with a compassionate expression on her face. "You tell me when you've spoken to your parents, then they can phone me directly, okay?"

I nodded. "Yeah, okay, I'm not ready yet, but when I do, I'll tell you, thank you."

"Of course," she said sweetly, as she left.

Just then, I felt my phone vibrate in my hand. Jamie had woken up and was responding to my updates throughout the night that I had sent him.

JAMIE: *God, infuriating that took so long. At least it got there in the end, don't worry. Have you improved since 5 am? Also, have you had the chance to speak to Jake? I'm happy to phone him if you don't want to.*

HEATHER: *I haven't slept at all, and I'm on my second bag of fluids. I can't eat either.*

JAMIE: *Don't ignore my Jake question, you bugger.*

I stared at the message. I wanted to be annoyed at Jamie for bringing Jake up, but the reality was, he should know by now. But, if I didn't have the courage to tell my parents yet, how could I even begin to tell the man I was in love with? Especially when the foundation of our relationship was based on honesty, and I had just lied by omission for an entire night about what was happening?

I closed my conversation with Jamie and opened up my one with Jake. The most recent messages between us included an affectionate, loving goodnight at around one in the morning when Jake would've been getting settled into bed after a long shift. He had no idea. He had no reason to think that anything would be wrong; our conversation yesterday had been the complete opposite of my one with Jamie. I felt sickened with my own blatant lies.

HEATHER: *Morning, baby. Look, I need to tell you something. I've been in the hospital since last night. I tried to kill myself. I'm so sorry I didn't tell you, but I didn't want to worry you when you were at work and so far away and not able to come and see me. I'm so sorry I lied to you. I only told Jamie, because he wasn't busy last night and I needed someone to talk to, and he eventually told Olivia because she might be coming to visit me today. I love you so much.*

It was a laughable message, and an awful way to break the news to my significant other of three years. I followed that text featuring my ridiculous outpouring of emotions with one containing the details of where I was, and what had been going on within the hospital, just to make sure he felt completely informed. I wasn't even sure if he was awake yet, but I suppose I'd be finding out soon.

Jamie texted me a second time, with nothing more than a question mark as he was waiting for my response.

HEATHER: *I'm waiting for his reply, you dick.*

JAMIE: *His reply? You should be ringing him.*

HEATHER: *Bruh.*

JAMIE: *Don't bruh me, bruh. C'mon.*

Jamie, yet again, was completely right. Which was a fact that deeply displeased me. I knew Jake deserved a phone call, and I knew that to text him was an inherently selfish act, much like many of the things I had been doing of late. More so, considering that I had at least graced Jamie with a verbal conversation.

Nevertheless, I knew I was completely incapable of handling a call with Jake right now. To hear his voice, and that level of concern would break my heart. To have to physically say the words "I tried to kill myself" to the person I loved above any other seemed like a Herculean task.

HEATHER: *You can phone him.*

JAMIE: *Okay, thanks.*

Just as I was about to send Jamie his number, Jake texted me back. My stomach sank.

JAKE: *Holy fucking shit, Heather. Why didn't you tell me? Baby, oh my god, I could have lost you last night. And I can't believe you're so far away. I wish you never went away, I wish I could see you, holy shit. I love you.*

HEATHER: *Jamie is going to phone you if that's okay? He can let you know what's going on. I'm not up to phoning right now. I love you, I'm sorry.*

JAKE: *Yes, of course.*

I sent Jamie the number and waited. It was all coming out now; people were starting to find out, and there was no going back. It was a terrifying feeling, especially when I was so sure I was not going to be facing this side of things. Especially when the future I did not think I was going to have was suddenly still present, and completely unpredictable.

I desperately did not want Jake to think he had any role to play in my decision, or that he had somehow failed in helping me over the past few years.

When I think back to the times when he would be holding me as I wept my way through a panic attack, or him picking up my medications for me because I was unfit to leave the house, only two thoughts come to my mind, *I am the most fortunate person to be with someone as thoughtful as him,* and, *his life would be so much easier without me.*

Which had been part of the reason why it had felt so easy to make the decision I did.

Whilst I waited for Jamie and Jake to finish what I was assuming was a very uncomfortable conversation, I figured I owed Olivia some updates too and sent her a copy of the report I had sent Jamie throughout the night. She replied almost immediately, to my comfort.

OLIVIA: *Thank you for sending that over. I'm gonna try to get to you today. What ward are you on, and what are the visiting hours?*

HEATHER: *Medical Assessment Unit. Room D. About 3.00–7.30 pm, but I obviously don't expect you to stay that long. Honestly, if you can't, don't worry.*

I already felt so eaten up about the struggles I had caused. I didn't want Olivia to feel obligated to visit and see me in my current state.

OLIVIA: *Okay, I'll be there. Did you sleep last night? Have you spoken to Ruaridh?*

HEATHER: *Thank you so much, this means so much to me, thank you. I haven't slept a wink, annoyingly. And no, I haven't told him. I want to, but I haven't.*

OLIVIA: *Try to rest, I'll speak to Ruaridh. Do you want anything brought later?*

HEATHER: *Let me know what happens. And Lucozade would be phenomenal. Please be warned I look like shit. I don't have a hairbrush so I haven't brushed my hair in, like, two days. I don't have my glasses so I can't see. I'm wearing two hospital gowns and don't have a toothbrush either.*

I added a laughing face at the end of the message. A pathetic attempt at lightening up a foul mood.

OLIVIA: *Ruaridh just wants you to know that he hopes you're okay. He has said he will come to visit you with me today if you want, but no pressure. And don't be silly, that stuff doesn't matter, I can grab you some stuff.*

HEATHER: *I'd like to see Ruaridh, yeah.*

OLIVIA: *I'll tell him.*

HEATHER: *Thank you. This is something to actually look forward to.*

The rain from outside was beginning to stop, and I found myself wondering what the weather was like back at home.

I noticed how easy it was for me to step out of my ongoing situation, and contemplate something as mundane as the weather. I found it satirical that I, the person at the epicentre of this earthquake, could so effortlessly *not* think about anything important. Whereas, I could guarantee that Jake, Jamie, Olivia and Ruaridh were not going to be thinking of anything else.

How insensitive did that make me? I was torn between apologising for every move I made and asking for help throughout this whole affair. Torn between trying to make myself the least problematic I can be, whilst simultaneously being exceedingly so.

I could almost hear Gaby saying, "That's classic Type Two behaviour!"

Gaby, my best friend, was wildly fun. She was the kind of person who would lead games of 'Truth or Dare?' at parties, which would leave you somewhere between drunk and crying as she asks questions about why you are the way you are or eating a raw egg as a bet. Any wild stories from these times usually began with Gaby initiating a drinking game of some form.

Despite being a hard-hitter during party games, she was also incredibly analytical and emotional. She would enjoy getting to know a person and getting into the depths of their motivations, feelings, fears and thoughts. Thus, when she discovered the Enneagram test, where you could find out which one of the nine personality types you are, she was hooked. We consequently spent a night with the Struggle maliciously learning which of us were which type, and that was when Gaby announced that I was a 'Type Two'.

Type Two people have one basic fear: being unwanted, or unworthy of love. Their basic desire could also be whittled down to one thing: to feel loved.

Alongside this, people like myself are motivated by similar things, such as the desire to be needed and appreciated. At our best, type two's are generous and helpful and feel at best being so. Doing good toward others is what makes them feel special. They can be compassionate, supportive, and every other positively defined word you could pull out of a dictionary.

However, if things go bad, it can get sour. Type two typically puts everyone else's care above their own. They let things like self-care slide, and become extremely self-depractive. They'll wear themselves out on behalf of every other person.

I was never one to typically believe in things like this. I could easily compare it to the likes of saying your personality is a direct relation to your star sign (another area of interest for Gaby, actually), yet, I could not deny how hauntingly truthful the description of a Type Two was to my own behaviours.

That moment when someone specifically says, "Heather, I need your help" or they make me feel validated and sought after, is like crack to me. It is no use to me for someone to say "I always appreciate you" because I'd rather have constant, and continual, reminders. Which made me high-maintenance, and I knew that. As with everything I do, I have a persistent level of self-knowledge, but no ability to stop any of the intrusive thoughts, impulsive behaviour, or invasive anxiety.

I would do anything for anyone but not for myself.

Logically, as many people with mental health illness probably know, I am not without love or support.

Within my college course, I had the company of Olivia, Jamie, Ruaridh, Ethan, Alistair, Connor and Kai.

At home, I had the Struggle, made up of Sam, Ben, Ryan, and Gaby.

Then, of course, I had Jake.

For all these people continually confirming my worth and their love toward me, you would almost think I could believe them, even marginally. But no. Because the voice in the back of my head says, *They're lying, they're saying it because they have to, you may as well die and stop burdening them*, will always drown out anyone else.

Depression was a cruel joke. Like Tinkerbell, I needed recognition to live. The difference between me and the pixie, however, was that once I was given what I needed, I'd doubt it and refuse to believe its sincerity, ending up feeling just as out of place as before.

Sometimes I wish I had a fundamental cause for the way I am. I could say, "Oh, I'm this way because my parents hated me" or "I had no friends", but I can't. Depression doesn't discriminate. I have had the world offered to me on a silver platter and I still wanted a way out.

My phone lit up once more; a sight that was becoming progressively more exacerbating. As I reached for it, I felt the chill of the wires from my heart monitor against my skin.

JAKE: *That's me off the phone with Jamie. He just told me everything that happened, we had a talk about you, and he told me his concerns and thoughts from this week. I thanked him a lot, he said he was really glad you phoned and stuff.*

HEATHER: *His thoughts for this week?*

JAKE: *He noticed you were quiet and a bit distant this week. He said he asked if you were okay a couple of times but didn't want to press it on you and annoy you.*

I decided to send Jamie a text too, thanking him for speaking to Jake, and asking how it went.

JAMIE: *He's calm, which is great. Just taking in the facts. Just wanted to talk to him rather than him having to read it off a screen, you know?*

I thanked him again, then went back to my conversation with Olivia, who was asking me if I wanted anything more than a drink. I still didn't have the stomach for eating, at least not now.

The next couple of hours passed in what felt like a settled pattern for me; hitting the nurse's button so either Beth would come and unhook my IV so I could go and pee, then returning to answer the various texts I got from Jamie, Jake and Olivia. And by the time I responded to them, I probably had to go to the bathroom again. The fluids were certainly hydrating me and flushing out anything adverse from my system, but I was resenting the season pass to the toilet that I currently had.

By noon, it was confirmed that Olivia and Ruaridh would indeed be visiting. Ruaridh would be leaving at around one o'clock from Wales, to get here by three, and Olivia was leaving around two o'clock. Despite my shame at them having to drop everything and make the journey, I was eager to see them. I needed a break from the monotony of lying in bed and being in pain.

JAKE: *Have you seen the mental health team?*

HEATHER: *I saw a doctor who patted me on the back. They mentioned someone speaking to me, but it might not be until tomorrow, they didn't say.*

JAKE: *Mental health care in hospitals is shite.*

At around 1 pm, just as Ruaridh texted me to say he was just leaving his house, Beth popped her head around the curtain to tell me that my blood work came back 'fine', whatever that meant. She offered me food, again, and I denied it again.

I merely put my headphones in, lay back, watched the fire escape door, and waited.

***

The curtains pulled back violently, and a tall, angry Welshman appeared in front of me.

"What the fuck did you do?" he demanded, a slight grin crept across his face as reassurance he wasn't actually attacking me.

A petite figure appeared behind him, smiling nervously as if she didn't know what to expect.

I laughed, shaking my head, and beamed at my two guests; Ruaridh and Olivia.

"Hey, guys." I tried to hide my enthusiasm, but I failed. Last night seemed like a year ago, and I was just so relieved to see two familiar faces.

Of course, I've always been told that regardless of how I am on the inside, I always act like I am on top of the world; I can't switch off. It's an argument I've yet to prove wrong. Maybe that is why people get taken aback when I open up about my depression. If you were to put me in a line-up, and select which person seemed the least held together; it wouldn't be the loud, smiling, extroverted person would it?

That's why depression is a silent killer; you never know who is hiding it until it's too late.

Ruaridh sat down somewhat triumphantly into the armchair to my left, leaving Olivia to pull up one of the ghastly plastic seats.

"Thank you so much for driving up guys, you honestly didn't have to."

"Shut up," Olivia said, "of course we came."

There was silence for a few seconds, as I felt them examine me. I couldn't blame them for being taken aback. I looked grim, quite frankly. I knew this despite not even looking in a mirror since being at the hotel. I could feel my greasy hair sticking to me, my eyes were raw and my skin was dry. And I probably reeked, too.

"Sorry about these bandages," I apologised yet again, "I know this is uncomfortable."

Ruaridh and Olivia refused to accept my remorse, their responses following along the lines of "Shut up".

The conversation that followed suit bounced between different topics; what happened, how shocked they were, and repeatedly asking if they could do anything for me.

"Can you fix my bladder so I stop peeing so much?" I joked, and nodded toward my IV drip, as I leaned over to push the nurse's button.

"I think this is the third one I've had and they want me to have around ten. I cannot stop pissing, it isn't even funny, I need to buzz for a nurse every time so they can unhook me from this drip."

I waved my arm in frustration, as my friends chuckled at my situation. Beth came back, and unhooked me, politely smiling at my friends. I might have been mistaken, but I'm sure Ruaridh perked up when he saw her, as she was undoubtedly very attractive.

I swung my legs around, to stand up, forgetting what happened when I moved, and when my hospital gown pulled up. I flushed red, and stood up hurriedly, pulling the robe down to cover my ugly, intensely cut thighs. But I knew it was too late, and Olivia and Ruaridh would have seen. It was too glaringly obvious to miss it. So I did what I always do; refused to acknowledge it, smiled, and walked away.

Once I had returned, and been hooked back up to the machine, the three of us began making small talk. It was pleasant, nothing to write home about, and it felt good to laugh. I think they understood that I didn't want the conversation topic to only be what I had just done the night before, and what was going to happen from here on out.

After Ruaridh had written 'cock' on the whiteboard above my bed, I began to talk about the hotel.

"All my stuff is still there. I don't know if I can go back and get it all. Plus, my glasses are there, and my underwear. I don't know what to do." I was aware of how gross I was, and how little I could see. It certainly wasn't helping my current mood.

"Well, we can go and get your things for you," Olivia offered.

"I can't let you do that." I shook my head. "You've already driven down here to see me, it isn't fair."

"Heather, do you want us to get your stuff for you?" Ruaridh said, firmly.

"If you don't mind," I admitted, sheepishly.

"Okay. We'll do that and get food for you too. Text us what you want. And if you could give us your hotel key too." Olivia ran through the game plan for me.

"Thank you so much." I realised my constant gratitude and apologies wore thin very quickly, but it wasn't like I was in a position to write a thank you card or anything.

Once they left to raid my hotel, I texted them a list of what I needed as Beth appeared at my bedside to change the IV.

"Are those your friends?" she asked politely.

"Yeah." I beamed. "Olivia drove an hour to see me, and Ruaridh drove two hours. I feel so bad for them, now they're going to my hotel to get my things for me."

Beth looked impressed. "Wow, that's so kind. They can stay as long as they want, don't worry about visiting hours." She winked as she left.

For someone whose life was full of so much internalised depression, self-loathing and negativity; I was surrounded by such kindness. Which made me the most selfish person around.

With Ruaridh and Olivia away on their voluntary errand run, I used the opportunity to tick off another box on my 'post suicide attempt to-do list', which was to tell my friends at home.

I was going to be going home to Scotland at some point. I wanted to make sure that, upon returning, my support wasn't entirely reliant on Jake. If I crashed and burned, I didn't want to set him ablaze because he was the only person trying to douse the fire.

I drafted together a simple message, detailing what had happened (minus any unsavoury parts), where I was, and stated that I was just telling them because I loved them, trusted them, and would be home soon and may need a support network. Once I got the seal of approval from Jake that the message sounded fair, I sent it to a few select people I felt close enough to open up to; Sam, Ryan and, of course, Gaby.

Messages began flooding in from the moment I hit 'send', and my inbox was beginning to fill with overwhelming positivity, from Sam and Ryan firstly.

SAM: *Omg, Heather, I don't know what to say, I'm so sorry man, I am so glad you're okay though, I don't know what I would do without you. You're incredibly brave for opening up and letting us know, legit, we love you so much, we are shit at showing it but you truly are an amazing person, we all need you in our life. You will always be the Struggle Queen, after all, you were the first girl we added to our group (by me, might I add). Heather, I am sorry you felt it had to come to that, it is so difficult for us in particular because of how busy we are, but legit, just know we all love you dearly and just wanna know you're safe.*

Sam seemed to be tripping over his words a bit, but it made me grin quite widely to myself.

RYAN: *Thanks for letting me know. I am ridiculously glad you contacted Jamie that night. You did fantastically. I know I don't do a good job of showing it 24/7 but just know I'm here for you if you need me in any capacity. I've set your number on my phone as a priority so if you ever need to contact me, it will ring through silent mode. I might not be able to do a massive amount in person but genuinely any time, day or night, rain or shine, I'm only a call or text away!*

Ryan's reply lightly surprised me. Unlike Sam and I, who regularly professed our love to each other, Ryan and I kept a mutual acknowledgement that we adored each other and didn't comment on it often. I wasn't sure what I was expecting within his response, but it was certainly more emotive than anticipated. I was touched.

Before I even had the chance to reply to either of them, Sam had sent me another flurry of messages, alongside a photo album. When I opened it, I saw numerous photos of him and I together; at parties, at pubs, on walks. They were all from over the past three years of our friendship. We looked so young in some of them, that it felt like a lifetime ago.

SAM: *Here are some photos of us to show how good our times together are, #drunkselfies. The last one is our first ever photo together, lol. I know it's rough right now, but just think of all the pictures we have yet to take. Just a little thing I thought would cheer you up.*

Somewhere, in the back of my mind, below the fog of depression, I knew they meant the words they were saying, but I could not accept that, which was part of the reason I was currently occupying a hospital bed. Part of my brain was screaming "They're saying this out of obligation!" at me, and I was listening to it.

I felt hypocritical for having some awareness of my problems, yet still giving into them. I felt selfish for wanting to remove myself from all the positivity being sent my way. I felt exhausted with the weight of fighting against my thoughts. And, at my core, I was just drained.

My phone buzzed, again. It was Gaby this time.

GABY: *Words cannot describe how proud I am of you. That must have been so terrifying and you are very brave for facing this. It is so great that you're making that effort to help yourself. I am really goddamn grateful to have you in my life and I can't wait until we are old ladies smoking cigars in the back garden. You are on my mind so often. This is the most loving friendship I've ever had and I am so glad it is with such a kind, curious and intelligent person. You've really shown me what being a best friend means. I have these moments where I am like 'Why is such a cool, pretty girl having out with me?' then you make me feel like a cool and pretty girl. I think that is evidence that you're an amazing human being.*

I had first met Gaby at my own eighteenth birthday party as a plus one of Ben's. She and Ben have been together for what feels like several lifetimes; they met as young teens and haven't left each other's side since. They're a beautiful couple, and to watch them simply be in love with each other is moving.

I remember the first time I saw her, and I was incredibly intimidated. Gaby is one of these fortunate individuals that look stunning naturally; she didn't need a single drop of make-up. She was immediately friendly, and you could instantly tell she was educated, talented and admirable.

When Gaby and I became friends, she admitted to me that she was equally intimidated by my presence at first.

According to her, I was the life of the party, and she was the shy girl standing in the kitchen with her boyfriend.

Now we were inseparable. I had had best friends before, but getting to be Gaby's confidant felt like something new, and better. I always cited Ryan's silly balloon film as giving me three great things; a boyfriend, a friend group and a best friend.

Depression is a cruel, hypocritical and nasty disease for not allowing these glowing positives to minimise anything awful in my life.

Ruaridh texted me, apologising for taking their time at the hotel, ending the message with a cryptic sentence implying that something had happened there.

HEATHER: *What happened? Was the hotel room cleaned?*

RUARIDH: *It was cleaned. But not very well.*

HEATHER: *What was still there?*

I hesitated before sending the message to him. I wasn't sure I wanted to hear the answer.

RUARIDH: *Patches of blood on the bed, carpet, blood in the fridge. A dismantled pencil sharpener with the blade next to it. Alcohol galore. A packet of matches, which confused us.*

I threw my head back on the pillow, and started up at the ceiling, swearing under my breath. Not only was I humiliated, but I felt somewhat villianish for having made two wonderful people feel they have to drive for hours to comfort me, then collect my belongings and give me food, and then view a scene straight out of a gory horror flick.

I had forgotten about the matches too. I did have every intention of using them. When I wasn't cutting, I would burn myself as a secondary way to harm myself. I would light the match, then put it out on my skin. It would smart, and immediately blister; a small, white circle of burnt skin that would gradually become more and more noticeable. I wasn't going to share that with Ruaridh, however.

I found myself wishing I had done this alone. Not for myself but for the sake of my loved ones.

Ruaridh and Olivia returned eventually and the hotel was not mentioned again. We simply ate, joked about them seeing my bras as they packed for me, commenting on the fact that they were push-up bras. I explained the problem with bigger breasts – like mine – is that they sag. I just wanted to help them out a bit before I became one of those old ladies who trip over them, so I liked to hoist them up a bit. I'm sure any girl with big boobs would understand.

They then began their separate journeys home, my constant thanks and apologies (and facts about my tits) still ringing in their ears.

About twenty minutes after Ruaridh and Olivia left, Beth came by to release me from my drip (how many bags of fluid had I had by now?) so I could go pee yet again. I sat on the toilet and looked down at my thighs. They looked almost akin to a tiger's fur; except instead of beautiful, black stripes, it was ugly, red cuts.

I ran my finger over them. They had been scabbing over quite quickly but were still a shocking shade of red, and quite swollen around the edges. However, I had a nasty habit of scratching myself, consequently reopening old wounds, and lengthening the healing process.

As my finger brushed over my skin, I began counting to myself.

One, two, three…

One hundred and seventy-seven times.

I had cut my thighs one hundred and seventy-seven times.

One hundred and seventy-seven; an odd number.

One hundred and seventy-seven; the second-highest score in darts.

One hundred and seventy-seven; the police emergency telephone number in Switzerland.

One hundred and seventy-seven; the number of scales depicted on a Chinese dragon.

One hundred and seventy-seven; the number of scars that would follow me for the rest of my life.

That wasn't even including my arms, which were bandaged right now; hidden from me. If I were to guess, it would bring my numbers up into the two-hundreds, easily.

I stood up, flushed, and splashed some water on my face. I felt the weight of the heart monitor as I leaned forward. I left the bathroom and was hooked back onto my drip.

I wasn't sure how to react to that number. One hundred and seventy-seven. I knew I should be crying, I should be remorseful and I should be horrified. But I felt nothing. I couldn't give myself permission to be upset, because I was the sole reason for this.

I could almost hear everyone exclaiming, "It isn't your fault! It's your mental health!"

There was some truth to that, my brain was clearly dysfunctional. It had given me epilepsy and depression; a buy one get one free deal. It had told me that the only way to escape the feelings I was having was to hurt myself.

And yet, I still couldn't help but blame myself. I simultaneously hated that I did this sickening stuff myself, whilst using it as a crutch for all these years. It was like I was being held up by a three-legged stool; if I were to take away a leg, without replacing it, I would fall over.

I needed to replace self-harm with a healthy coping mechanism, to keep myself held up. But I had yet to find that replacement. Whenever you bring up the topic of self-harm to people, you hear the same advice over and over. "Have you tried the elastic band technique?", "Have you tried drawing on yourself with a red pen?" and the always popular, "Have you tried putting ice on your arm?"

Yes, yes and yes. I had tried it all. People who are fortunate enough to not have experienced this gorier side of depression just simply cannot understand why people like me do it. They also can't understand that most of us try everything possible to *not* hurt ourselves, but the overwhelming urge takes you over.

Most people don't understand, and I can't find the words to explain why I have to do it.

My phone buzzing, yet again, broke me out of my daydream. Jamie had sent me a link to the song, *You're the Best* by Joe Esposito.

HEATHER: *Sarcasm?*

JAMIE: *Absolutely not.*

The ward was quiet, much similar to when I had first arrived. I heard the hushed voices of nurses at the other side of my curtains, and the patter of their shoes against the linoleum floors. It was late, and patients were likely already drifting off, but the staff's night wasn't ending just yet. For me, it felt like an increasingly never-ending day, and I doubted I would sleep much tonight, if at all. Too many thoughts were scrambled in my head, and I couldn't relax enough to doze off comfortably.

In the morning, I would have to tell my parents. That was a task that gave me pangs of anxiety just thinking about it. I pushed that thought as far back in my mind as I could.

I'd also have to handle college tomorrow. Do I go home instead of staying next week? How much time do I take off? Should I drop out entirely?

I was smart. Or, at least, I was selectively smart. Maths and Science? I was horrible at them. But subjects like English, Drama, and Social Sciences? I adored them.

That was why I wanted to study media and eventually work in it. Above all, I loved telling stories; whether it be fiction or nonfiction. Growing up, I poured out short stories, most of them following a boy called Eddie and his pet unicorn. I branched into my young journalistic side as well and wrote a fake family newsletter entitled, *Thompson News*, detailing the very boring goings-on of my house. I was quite a pretentious child. This was a quality I still retain, depending on who you ask.

The area of media I wanted to be in changed a lot growing up, from journalist to editor, camera operator to director. Finally, I realised the reason I was unable to narrow down my choices was that it all interested me. As long as I was contributing to storytelling, it didn't matter what area I wound up in; writing, television, radio, film – anything.

That mentality would eventually open a lot of doors for me if I hadn't been continually demolishing my further education opportunities. It began with my repeated absence at school, followed by dropping out of university after four months. And now I was on this college course; a door I may have just closed behind me.

University had felt too much for me. A combination of long days, not fitting into any group or clique, and having to do eight mandatory classes (of which only three were media-related) was too overwhelming for me. I thought that my current course would be manageable; a lesser but more specific qualification, part-time study, and only eight other students. But here I was.

And yes, I could put the responsibility of these blunders on my mental health. Depression was venomous. Yet, I couldn't help but feel that I had given up too easily. That my inability to handle such things was due to failure on my part, and not the symptoms of my illness. I was letting my depression win.

I turned over in my bed. Somewhat. There was only so much comfort I could have right now, physically and emotionally.

It isn't until you're in a hospital bed, under thin white blankets, lying on a plastic, crunching mattress, that you truly appreciate your bed at home. At the very least, if I was home, I'd have a small ball of fur lying with me in the form of my cat, Coco.

Coco was the greatest. She was small, tiny for her older age of thirteen. She was a beautiful mixture of grey and ginger, which split almost evenly on her face. As she got older, her meows grew squeaker, and more continuous. But I didn't mind.

She was exceedingly needy – something I could relate to – and followed me from room to room whenever I was home. When I was in bed, she crawled all over me, squeaking and meowing, drooling slightly the happier she was. She'd curl up into a ball, emanating heat and vibrating slightly as she purred, and lie under my duvet at the bend of my knees. Every night, without fail.

I wasn't a crazy cat lady, by any means. But your pet is your pet, and Coco was wonderful. I had had her in my life longer than any of my friends when I thought about it. She was a gift to me when I was seven years old, and she was only six weeks old. Since then, Heather and Coco had been kicking it up together.

The more I thought about her absence at the end of my bed, the colder it felt.

Although, I suppose, everything felt cold and lonely right now.

Sunday

It was about 8.30 am. I had about three hours of sleep. Now that Jake and my friends knew, I had to do the bit I had been putting off the most; telling my parents. There was no more avoiding it, and if I wasn't going to tell them, I knew someone else would do it soon, in the name of 'looking out for me'.

I couldn't phone them. It was just like when I told Jake. I couldn't handle hearing their voices. The disappointment, the tears, and all the questions I didn't have answers for right now. I was just going to send a text. A cop-out, maybe, but at least I could spend the time to word it perfectly. The bliss of modern technology; allowing us to avoid any real confrontations.

I sat, looking at my phone for what felt like an age before I thought, *Fuck it*, and composed the message that would change everything. As this would be sent to my parents, I had to ensure I had as much information about where I was as possible, to minimise concern. Although, I suppose, other people's emotions were quite out of my control right now. God, I was a shit person.

A small mercy was the existence of my family group chat, containing my mum, dad and I, meaning that I didn't have to get in touch with them individually.

HEATHER: *Okay, so I have something to tell you guys and sorry but you won't like it. And please don't phone me, only text, as I cannot handle phone calls right now. I've been in hospital since 8 pm on Friday, and I am still here, due to a suicide attempt. I won't share the details of what I did, but I'll tell you what's been happening since.*

On Friday, I phoned Jamie and told him what I had done. An ambulance was called (I was in the hotel at this point, my colleagues had gone home) and Jamie stayed on the phone with me whilst I waited for it. He then texted me until 2 am to make sure I was okay. He is also my emergency contact for this hospital. He also phoned Jake on Saturday and told him what had happened, because I hadn't told him.

I have been admitted into a Medical Assessment Unit, which means there are six of us, and two nurses stay in the ward just monitoring us. So whenever I need anything I immediately get it. I've had three 8-hour bags of fluid, I'm on my fourth right now. I've had 4 blood tests and a thumb prick test. I've had 2 swabs done and two CG exams. I've had a 24-hour heart monitor on since 2 pm yesterday. I also get my temperature and blood pressure taken regularly. And I have been bandaged where I need to be.

The staff are utterly phenomenal, so welcoming and helpful, and they knew I was by myself and from Scotland, so they went out of their way to make me feel at home. Yesterday, Olivia and Ruaridh drove to visit me. They also went to the hotel and collected all my stuff and brought me food. I'm getting out this afternoon.

In terms of actual physical health, I've felt better. On Friday they were worried because I had stomach cramps, nausea, uncontrollable shaking and my pupils were huge. Saturday, I was nauseous and had a raised temperature. Today I'm just sore where my self-harm is and nauseous. I'm not eating much but trying. Only really had a few hours of sleep though.

Again, please do NOT phone me. I wouldn't even let Jake phone me. Just text. I didn't tell you sooner because I had a lot to deal with and needed time to sort out some arrangements and process everything. I love you.

I read what I had written, over and over, until the words had burned their way into my memory. I sighed slowly and added a small paragraph with details about where I was, what ward I was in, and about Beth's offer from yesterday regarding them phoning her, complete with her number she had given me earlier.

I locked my phone and sat it far away from me, trying to convince myself that if I wasn't looking at my phone, I could put off dealing with anything else.

However, even I couldn't ignore the sight of my phone screen lighting up out of the corner of my eye, as someone messaged me back.

DAD: *Your mum isn't awake yet. I don't know what to say at the moment other than I love you. Will text you in a wee bit.*

My shoulders relaxed a bit, as I exhaled a breath I didn't know I was holding and felt relatively eased. He hadn't said much – which didn't surprise me, what would you say to a message like that? He was likely shocked but it was a response I could handle. It wasn't brimming with guilt trips or questions; just a tactful acknowledgement and some love.

HEATHER: *Okay. I love you.*

It was only about half an hour before my mum woke up, however, and messaged too.

MUM: *How are you now?*

My mum's texts always came across as a bit blunt, but she wasn't particularly an enthusiastic texter, so I, like the rest of my family, learned not to assume she was always angry. That's just what happens when our parents begin to use technology, I guess.

HEATHER: *Just done physically and emotionally. I've been in hospital for three days, glad to be getting out today.*

MUM: *I just want to shake you and hug you at the same time. Your dad is going to phone your nurse.*

HEATHER: *Okay, let me know how it goes.*

I lay back on my bed. It was all out now, no taking it back. Everything was different now. I was now the girl who tried to kill herself, in everyone's eyes. I couldn't even begin to imagine what my parents would be like when I got home.

It was both unusual and not unexpected that it took me so long to tell my parents. Unusual in that I am incredibly close with both of them, and we had an open-book relationship. But that was the very reason why I held off; I knew that when I told them, they would begin asking questions, "But you tell us everything, why didn't you tell us you were struggling this badly sooner?" Hypocrisy, thy name is Heather.

I think the best parts of me were a direct combination of my parents' influences.

My mother was a beautiful woman, in every way possible. She worked as a carer, helping those with disabilities in their day-to-day life. She was educated and poured her spare time into reading. She passed that epic love for books onto me, and I was so grateful for that. We swapped reading lists and would talk for hours over our favourite authors and stories. We marched into book festivals with a level of unmatchable excitement, as we listened to hours of different authors' talks and waited in queues to get books signed.

But more than that, she was determined, powerful and unstoppable. She was, to me, the definition of an exceptional woman.

My dad was my hero. He was a design draughtsman by day and the coolest person at night. Despite being in his late forties, he played in a few local grind and noise core bands as the bassist. It was undoubtedly my dad's influence that made me want to be a musician. He went to horror movie festivals, was still getting tattoos, and rocked one outfit; dad shorts and band t-shirts. He was utterly unapologetically himself and didn't give a fuck about anyone's opinion.

It was a great attitude to be around.

I felt my phone vibrate in my hand as my dad replied.

DAD: *It went fine, she had a great manner and was very reassuring. I think she could tell how worried I was. She filled me in with what you did/what happened (I'm not sure if you'd feel right/comfortable with me writing it down in a message) and that a mental health specialist will be around to see you this afternoon. She seemed pleased with your recovery so far.*

HEATHER: *She's bloody lovely, makes me feel so relaxed.*

DAD: *It makes a massive difference when you click with someone.*

MUM: *Are you getting discharged today?*

HEATHER: *Yes.*

MUM: *You know you can always talk to us, right?*

DAD: *Heather, I can come get you tonight and I am willing to drive you home. I'll talk to your college course leader and explain the situation. You shouldn't be staying in England for another week.*

HEATHER: *Dad, that's like six hours down here then six hours back.*

DAD: *I don't care. We can take a break every few hours and we can listen to music too.*

HEATHER: *Thank you so much. I love you. When will you be leaving then?*

DAD: *About 3 pm. I'd get there around 9 pm.*

HEATHER: *I'll be discharged before then. I can go back to the hotel I was meant to be staying in next week. You could get me there, then?*

DAD: *Sounds like a plan. I love you. See you soon.*

I checked the time. It was 2.30 pm now.

Whilst I was completely speechless at what my dad was so selflessly doing for me, the guilt was slowly eating away at me. Not only had I just caused some emotional earthquakes in the lives of my loved ones, but now my dad was about to make a twelve-hour journey just to pick me up because I couldn't even be trusted to head home alone.

If I were to be honest with myself, I didn't wholly believe that I deserved the unconditional support I got from my parents. During my time in high school, I was a different person; an angry, unpredictable person. This didn't come out during school time, but rather when I was home. I took all the hurt and pain I didn't know how to share and manifested it into lashing out at my, frankly, undeserving parents.

I would slam doors, pick arguments at any opportunity and scream the house down. I was confused and didn't know how to deal with my flawed mental health. I didn't know how to reach out, especially after my one attempt resulted in my friend telling me that "other people have real problems". The only thing I knew how to do was to be furious at the world. I took that fury, and ignorance on how to open up, and used it to further fuel the fire that was my self-harm and eating disorder.

That wasn't to say I was always uncontrollably hostile, because I wasn't; it was not a 24/7 situation. I've always gotten along with my parents, despite those difficult few years. However, it took me a significant amount of time to reach that point. I eventually took the anger away from those around me, and targeted it inward, toward myself. Since that point, I have desperately tried to apologise to my parents through changed behaviour, but I was never truly sure if they knew how remorseful I felt.

Yes, depression made you indescribably down. But it also had a way of making you equally enraged.

A lot of my behaviour embarrassed me. Whether it be my anger from years ago or the person I've become now. When I am being too loud, sharing something about myself, or opening up about my mental health, I just want to shrink into myself. I want to disappear, but for some reason, I am incapable of stopping. Even if I am moulding myself into someone I *think* other people would like, I still cringe at myself.

Neither the real me nor the fake me were good enough.

I text Jake, who had been fretting about how I was getting home all day.

HEATHER: *My dad is coming to pick me up. It'll be a twelve-hour-long trip.*

JAKE: *Oh really? Well, that's a relief that your dad will be there.*

It was a relief, yes. But I didn't feel like a person anymore. I felt like a burden; a poison that was contaminating those trying to help me. I take up too much space in my friends' lives.

One decision I made that I failed to carry through, had caused everyone to drop everything. I felt selfish, and forever indebted to each one of them.

I didn't have time to dwell on my guilt for long, however, before Olivia texted me.

OLIVIA: *Have you told Leigh yet about what is going on? If not myself, Ruaridh or Jamie can speak to her.*

HEATHER: *Fuck. No. I haven't. Yes, please, can you tell her? Thank you so much.*

OLIVIA: *No worries, I just want to help.*

Leigh was our main college lecturer, who ran the course, and was our go-to for anything we needed. We often joked that she was our college mum, but that description honestly wasn't too far off. She was a warm lady, who you felt comfortable being around. She certainly did watch over us like a proud mother hen. She made a difficult and complicated course that bit easier.

She did have a stern talk with me once, however, about my dark Scottish humour. Maybe 'stern talk' was too harsh. But she did very pointedly say to me, "Remember, not all your colleagues are Scottish, so they don't have the same dark sense of humour you do", oops.

I was, again, feeling the same nervousness I did when I was waiting for my parents and friends to respond to the news. That waiting game where you have no idea what is going to happen next. I couldn't believe I had done something so stupid as to forget to keep Leigh informed. I had been so caught up in trying to get home, telling my loved ones and peeing every ten minutes that I had completely failed to speak to the lady who was essentially running my college career. I sat, staring at my phone, drumming my fingers on the back of it until, eventually, an email popped up.

From: Leigh Wilson <l.wilson@cgu-coll.com>
To: Heather Thompson <h.thompson@cey.net>
Subject: Arrangements for next week.

Heather,

Olivia has informed me about what has happened and mentioned you were not up for many phone calls at the moment. I just want to extend you my greatest support, and to let you know you are welcome to take a break from college and recuperate at home.

Are you being discharged today? Do you have a means of getting home?

Best wishes,

Leigh.

From: Heather Thompson <h.thompson@cey.net>
To: Leigh Wilson <l.wilson@cgu-coll.com>
Subject: RE: Arrangements for next week.

Hey Leigh,

Sorry, you had to find out from other people. Yes, I'm not up to phone calls, so I appreciate your email. I am getting discharged this afternoon. I'm speaking to a mental health doctor first. My dad is driving down to get me at about 9 pm, so I can go home. I can give you my nurse or my mum's number if you want to speak to someone about it in more detail?

Cheers,
Heather.

From: Leigh Wilson <l.wilson@cgu-coll.com>
To: Heather Thompson <h.thompson@cey.net>
Subject: RE: RE: Arrangements for next week.

I have your mother's details in your emergency contact file, so I'll call her for a chat tomorrow if I have your permission to do so.

I'm glad that travel home has been sorted. We can cover your father's travel expenses for you. Please, of course, take a sabbatical from college. You spend the next week at home, then I'll phone you a week on Monday if that suits you and we can discuss a plan for you coming back to us. No pressure, of course, put yourself first. We also have access to college counsellors, which I can tell you a bit more about when we talk.

If you haven't informed the other students, would you like me to? If I do, what would you like me to say, would you rather I just said that you spent some time in hospital, or would you like me to share why you were there?

Best wishes,
Leigh.

From: Heather Thompson <h.thompson@cey.net>
To: Leigh Wilson <l.wilson@cgu-coll.com>
Subject: RE: RE: RE: Arrangements for next week.

Thank you for your help and understanding. I'm happy to phone you in a week and get a game plan on the go.
I'm also okay with you telling the others about why I am in the hospital. I trust them, I just don't have the energy to tell them myself at the moment.

Thanks again,
Heather.

From: Leigh Wilson <l.wilson@cgu-coll.com>
To: Heather Thompson <h.thompson@cey.net>
Subject: RE: RE: RE: RE: Arrangements for next week.

I'll take the time to phone them individually and tell them the situation.
Of course, please keep me updated, and let me know that you get home safely.
Thank you for your honesty. I'll speak with your mother tomorrow, and speak to you in a week.

Take care of yourself and do not worry about college at all. That can wait.

Best wishes,
Leigh.

So that was that. Once Leigh told the rest of my college group, everyone would know. My friends, my parents, Leigh and Jake. For the first time, nothing was hidden; it was all out in the open. I took a shaky breath as a wave of anxiety washed over me. Everyone was going to view me differently. I was the person who tried to kill herself. I wasn't Heather anymore. I was the person you'd text behind their back about saying things like, "Oh my God, did you hear Heather tried to kill herself?"

I wasn't Heather anymore. I was a failed statistic.

My curtain, keeping me in my own corner of the world, was pulled back yet again; like a play on its second act. But no one here was waiting for Godot or having affairs with their maid. There was only me, trying hard to remember the next lines in a script that was still being written.

A man, who I assumed was my hospital-appointed one-off therapist, smiled at me as he pulled the curtain back over behind him.

He looked young, maybe in his mid-thirties. His casual demeanour was somewhat relaxing, as he wore a red tartan shirt, accompanied with jeans. He also had slightly unruly blonde hair, which was clearly winning a war against hair gel.

"Heather, is it? I'm Marcus, I'm in the mental health team."

He shook my hand. The coolness of his palm highlighted the clamminess of mine. I'd need a shower as soon as I got back to the hotel, before the drive home. I hadn't showered since Friday, which seemed like a lifetime ago.

"Hi, yeah, thank you for coming." I returned his smile.

Marcus sat down on the chair Ruaridh had sat in yesterday. He looked down at his clipboard, which was full of notes about me, presumably.

"So, you're getting home today, where is it you'll be going?"

"Scotland. My dad is driving down to get me."

Marcus raised an eyebrow. This was clearly news to him, as he said, "Ah! Okay, I won't bother trying to organise follow-up care, that'll need to be dealt with when you get back by your local mental health crisis team."

He paused, then sat the clipboard on his knees, clapped his hands together, and leaned forward as if about to reveal a big secret to me.

"To be honest," he admitted, looking apologetic, "there is no point, really, in me being here. I can't put anything in place for you or get in touch with anyone in Scotland. That's going to be on you when you return home. Do you think that's something you're going to do?"

"Yeah," I said softly, almost so delicately it was like I had sighed, "yeah, I will, I want to."

"Good." Marcus sat back, satisfied. "Well, since I am here, let's just talk."

I'm sure he wanted me to say something at that point, maybe start the conversation, but what could I say? What could I condense into an opening sentence that encapsulates my years of pain for this person I'm never going to see again?

"What did you do a couple of days ago?" Marcus sensed my hesitation and broke the silence.

"I drank and overdosed on some medications I'm prescribed. I also cut, a lot."

"I noticed the bandages. And what happened to make you want to do this to yourself?"

I snorted quite loudly at that, taking the therapist by surprise, "I hate that question."

"Why?"

"Because it isn't just one singular event that made me think, 'Right, time to off myself'. It's years and years of many things, building up continually until it just reaches that point" – I was ranting quite passionately, much to my own surprise – "It isn't like a light switch moment. Nothing of note happened this week, at all. It just felt like time."

Marcus nodded, acknowledging my frustration. "I know, it's quite a vague question. You say that there have been things going on for years, so you have a history of feeling like this? Of suicide?"

"I've been depressed since I was around fourteen years old, give or take. The suicidal thoughts have been a more recent development, maybe just the past year or two. I've always had issues with self-harm." I laughed, perhaps due to my nervousness about opening up, or embarrassment at my own woefulness. "It used to be daily. I'm not even joking when I say that. I'd be doing it in the bathrooms in between classes, and every single night. That's died off a bit more recently, but still enough to be an issue, I suppose."

I was acutely aware that the only thing separating myself and Marcus from the rest of the ward was a piece of hanging fabric. The older patients around me were hearing all the gossip about my life. If I had been home, in my local hospital, with the possibility of someone recognising me, I would have demanded more privacy. But, I was a stranger to this place and a stranger that was just about to leave, at that. There was no reason to be bashful now.

"You say nothing of note happened this week. Why are you in England? Are you on holiday?"

I was surprised at the lack of briefing Marcus got before meeting me, but explained nonetheless.

"I come here for college sometimes. There are nine of us on my course, from across Britain, so usually, we are based at home. But sometimes we come to England together for a couple weeks. Instead of flying home just to fly back again, I was going to stay by myself in a hotel over the weekend. My college friends all live reasonably near, so they did go home, bar one guy. The other two Scots are staying at the houses of other students."

"So you were alone, in another country, in a hotel, for the weekend," Marcus said, piecing together what I had yet to say, "so that's why you decided now?"

I smiled sadly. "Pretty much. It was the perfect chance."

"Was it an impulsive decision?"

I considered this. "I want to say yes and no. I've always had a method I was going to use, but I'd set the date about a week before, which I suppose isn't too long in the future. I remember waking up and feeling so sure about it."

"What did Friday morning feel like for you?"

"I was anxious, and nervous, of course. But I still felt, like inherently calm. I remember this moment just sitting having lunch with some of my friends, and I just sat and watched them, thinking that it'll be the last time I'll see them, but I just felt nostalgic, more than anything. Not sad. Sad that I would miss them becoming successful people, but not sad that I was intending to, you know, die."

"So, what made you phone for help?"

"I feel like I know the answer to that, but I can't quite word it. I began to feel scared, especially when I saw the blood loss. I began to feel guilty, for the person who would have to find me. I was dizzy from everything and just began to feel so unsure of myself. Which pisses me off."

"Why does it piss you off?"

"Because when I had decided to attempt, I felt so peaceful. So *sure.* I knew all my issues were going to end. Then the minute I had the chance to do something, I doubted everything, and I'm not even totally sure why so now I've just upset everyone for absolutely no reason."

"And what have people been saying to you?"

"Everyone has been lovely. Asking after me, reminding me they love me. My friend, Sam sent me every single picture we have ever taken together, to 'remind me of the good times we have'." I grinned.

Marcus laughed. "That is quite sweet. Do you think they'll be supportive when you get home? Can you rely on them?"

I gritted my teeth, thinking carefully about how to word my answer.

"Technically, yes," I said, slowly, elongating my words, "but I'm worried. I think that my college friends will assume I'm getting all the necessary support from my boyfriend, my friends at home, and my family, so they'll step back. Then my Scottish friends will assume I'm getting help from my parents, medical teams, and my boyfriend. But if I'm home, and on a waitlist for therapy, it'll be just my boyfriend and I, and I hate myself for putting that all on him. I mean, I have my parents, of course, but that's a different sort of relationship, with only so much I'm willing to share."

"That is a perfectly sensible and valid worry," Marcus assured me, "how did your boyfriend react?"

"I'm not wholly sure," I admitted, "my friend Jamie had to phone him and explain the situation. He says that Jake, my boyfriend, was quite reserved when he spoke to him. I asked Jake, and he said he just didn't want to show his feelings to Jamie. He's been amazing, though."

"How long have you been together?"

"Just over three years."

"Long time."

"Yeah, it's been great."

I paused and grabbed a cup of water off my bedside table. The water was room-temperature by now, and incredibly disgusting, but my throat was dry and I needed a few seconds to pause and collect myself.

All Marcus was doing was asking short, simple questions, and giving me room to speak. It was especially relieving; I felt no pressure, and he wasn't making assumptions about me. Just an uncomplicated pattern of question, answer, question, answer. He was the first person I had spoken to all weekend about what was going on that didn't have a personal bias toward me beforehand, and it was a welcome change. Even if I would only see him today, on this one occasion, he was at least getting enough weight off my shoulders for me to feel able enough to leave the hospital, and travel home.

I wasn't sure if Marcus was asking me the questions I needed to be asked right now, and I wasn't sure if the answers

I were giving were the answers I wanted to give. A lot of questions were being thrown to me recently, and I had got used to regurgitating copy and pasted answers to all queries. Regardless, at this moment, it was helping to just speak with this gentleman who was being paid to sit and listen to me. Like a prostitute who satisfied your emotional needs, not your sexual ones.

"So, what does the future look like for you now?" Marcus asked. I considered this.

"That's a tough one to answer," I admitted, "considering up until Friday night, I didn't think I was going to be in possession of a future."

"But now that you do have one," Marcus pressed, "what would you want to do with it?"

"Well," I began slowly, "I suppose I should start with getting better. I'm not saying that I'll never get to a point where I want to end my life again, but right now that need is flushed out of my system, for lack of a better term. I suppose I'll go home, take some time out of college, get into therapy and on better medication, maybe."

"You misunderstand me." Marcus waved his hand. "I mean in three or so years' time."

"That's even harder." I laughed, "I guess. Finish college, get a good job in an area I love, probably either in the media or something to do with books. Marry Jake, and move in with him. Cat and dog. Keep in touch with my friends. No kids, never really fancied that idea. Get control of my seizures so I can get my driving license back. Travel, a lot. Get a lot of tattoos, too."

Marcus smiled. "Seems like life has a lot more to offer than you realised."

"That's the thing," I protested, "it's all very well to say this stuff, and recite the same old ideals everyone has for their life. But I can't imagine it happening, I can't comprehend it. It's one thing to say, 'Yeah this would happen' and another thing to have it. I can't imagine having that, it isn't a possibility for me."

"I think you doubt yourself too much, and you don't give yourself enough credit," Marcus said, "you're assuming this can't happen for you because you don't believe in yourself."

Marcus was right, and it struck a chord even more so that we had just met and he had noticed this. My inability to put myself first was someone most, if not all, of the people in my life had noticed. I would light myself on fire to keep others warm. I had tried to view my suicide attempt as something I was doing for myself, but I couldn't pretend that a big factor in my decision-making wasn't the idea that I would be ultimately helping everyone else in my life, by removing myself.

It felt like a weird concept; trying to imagine a future I didn't originally think I was going to have. Today was not a day I had intended to see. I had no firm plans for three days from now, let alone three years.

It was like I had written a book, and concluded it in a manner that was satisfactory for me. But then my agent turned around and told me I had to write a sequel. But I had no plot, and I thought the story had ended.

On Friday, and even during Thursday night, everything felt so finalised and complete. I didn't need to watch what I ate for dinner because I was trying to lose weight; I was going to die later. I didn't need to worry about finding a job when I completed college, because I wasn't finishing college in the first place. I didn't need to worry about my loved ones being happy because the burden of helping me would be lifted off, and they could move on.

Now I had a whole lifetime ahead of me to figure out, on top of dealing with the consequences of my weekend actions.

It was a nauseating thought.

"What about hobbies? Do you have anything to keep you busy while you take some time off college?"

"Yeah, I play in a brass band."

"Oh! What do you play?"

I laughed and prepared myself for his shocked reaction. "I play the tuba, actually."

Marcus's eyes widened. Every single time I told someone this, they were shocked. I was aware that I didn't look like a stereotypical tubist. I didn't wear flat caps, I wasn't morbidly obese, I wasn't a loner and, most notable, I wasn't male.

I had no shame playing a traditionally masculine instrument. Firstly, it's made my arms particularly strong from lugging about a huge case and tuba every week. Secondly, it made me feel incredibly powerful when I blasted a monstrous note on my E-flat bass. I'm biased, but bass instruments have always been superior to me.

I played with a local brass band, about thirty people, give or take. We had four tubists, including myself. The other three were men, as usually expected. I had only met one other female tubist in all my years as a musician.

I had joined the band when I was nine, making it a full eleven years I had been part of the community. They had watched me grow up, and go through all phases of my life, including when I chopped my hair off into an awful pixie cut.

I had originally joined as a trumpet player, using an old second-hand one that had once been my dad's. After about five years, there was a demand for more lower brass instrumentalists, and they offered to give anyone willing to learn one of them a brand new instrument.

Whilst I was happy whilst using a trumpet, I offered to make the change. And I am forever pleased that I did, as it clicked immediately with me. I adored how I could simultaneously be very intense, whilst adding my own feminine flare to a particularly masculine section of the band.

"That's an interesting one," Marcus commented.

"Yeah, I love it. Every Tuesday night for eleven years. A good few concert throughout the year too."

Talking about my band would always remind me of some special moments with my grandpa, oddly enough. Whenever my dad had to work late, it was Grandpa who drove me to and from band practice on a Tuesday night. We had great conversations, and honest talks, where he would tell me things he wouldn't in front of Gran. Sometimes it would be advice about fighting, "Someone's going to fight you? Hit them first on the chin, then boot them" or driving, "Cyclist on the road? Run them over" or even a retelling of a childhood story, "So this boy was making a fool out of me in school, so I broke his nose with my arm cast. No one makes a fool out of me."

So there were a few positives of being a musician, and some were unexpected.

"And how do you feel when you're performing?"

I didn't need a moment of consideration to answer this.

"I feel fantastic. When I perform, absolutely nothing comes to mind bar music. I get absorbed in the sheet music, and listening to everyone playing, and noticing how we all fit together and create some, frankly, awesome sounds."

"Do you think you're talented?"

"I think I'm alright. I have nothing on my bandmates." I shrugged nonchalantly.

"You're putting yourself down again." Marcus pointed out.

I laughed a little. "You would too if you were me."

"Is there any person out there that would agree with how you talk about yourself?"

Probably every human ever, I thought bitterly. I decided to offer up a different answer to Marcus.

"I hope not. I try to please everyone I meet. I guess I'll alter myself to fit their dynamic, to try and get them to like me. No matter how I feel, I try my best to come across like a good person. A friend."

"And why do you do that?"

I hesitated.

"Because I don't want people to see me the way I see myself," I said feebly.

"How do you see yourself?" Marcus asked, continuing his mantra of short, simple, yet poignant questions.

"Annoying. Needy. Loud. Intense. Ugly. High-maintenance." I bit my lip. "I could go on."

"I want you to do something for me." Marcus sat back and clicked on a pen; the only noise that had come through during our conversation. "I want you to list five things you like about yourself."

"I'm not sure I can do that," I said shortly, giving Marcus a look that hopefully read like "Please don't make me do this".

129

"I'm serious." Marcus smiled gently. "You find it so easy to talk about yourself in such a negative way. I want to see what positives you can come up with."

I thought about this, longer than I had any other question the special guest therapist had asked me.

"I like my body modifications. My piercings and tattoos, I think they're pretty sweet," I began. Marcus nodded.

"What's your favourite modification?" he asked.

"My septum ring. The first body modification I got, bar getting my ears pierced. Got it on my sixteenth birthday and, other than changing the jewellery, I've never had it out."

I remembered how adult I felt after getting my septum pierced. I had to have parental permission to get it done if I was under sixteen, and my parents understandably refused. So when my birthday hit, I was out the door like a shot, and went and got one. I had got lost on the way to the piercing studio, and awkwardly bumped into my ex-girlfriend, Robyn. Having to have that uncomfortable "how are you, how's things, we should catch up soon" conversation did not add any positivity to my birthday celebrations.

It had been my first time in a piercing and tattoo parlour, and I was certainly a bit intimidated. Although, I suppose anyone would be when a bearded, heavily tattooed man was leaning over to shove a needle through your nose.

It hurt, but not more than I expected. My eyes had watered so extensively that my eyeliner washed off. I had tear streaks down my cheeks, and blood dripping out my nose, over my lips and down my chin. But I loved the rush of it.

Either my parents warmed up to the horseshoe ring through my nose, or they stopped caring about it. Regardless, piercings became such a part of me that most people in my life had never seen me without them in; including Jake, who said he probably wouldn't like it, because it wouldn't be 'me'.

"What else do you like about yourself?" Marcus pressed.

"I like that I'm a musician. I like that I can read sheet music fluently, it's a cool skill."

"That is cool." Marcus nodded in agreement. "I couldn't do that, it all means nothing to me. Has there been any song you've performed that you particularly enjoyed?"

I smiled. "Fuck, yeah. A few years ago we did the 'War of the Worlds' suite. The Peter Graham arrangement. The first movement is called Wrath and it's very tuba heavy, and just sounds so mighty."

It had been, at least for me, the most complicated piece of music I had played at that point. The entire suite was around twenty minutes long, with five movements in it. It depicted the entire story of aliens arriving on Earth, through to the war and eventual rebuilding of society.

However, I didn't care about the backstory as much as I cared about the tuba part. As a bass instrument musician, tubists resign themself to a playing career of one of two banal pieces; crotchet, rest, crotchet, rest or about eight semibreves in a row. So when you're given a piece that breaks that monotony, you understandably become ecstatic.

Marcus laughed. "Okay, third thing you like about yourself?"

"I guess third would be that I'm a reader. I've read more books than anyone I know. Well, anyone bar my mum. I really like to read, I'm well versed."

I felt like I was vainly bragging about myself. I wasn't used to talking about myself in this manner and I was in slight discomfort. I couldn't shake the feeling of sounding boastful.

Marcus was pushing me to answer his questions, and the logical part of me knew that he wasn't viewing me as arrogant. Yet, I wasn't wholly enjoying this process.

"What are your favourite books?" Marcus asked.

"I'm always looking for new recommendations."

"Oh, well, A Clockwork Orange is my favourite." I didn't like being put on the spot like this and had to think momentarily before I pulled more suggestions out. "Animal Farm is up there. Johnny Got His Gun was weird but good."

"A lot of classics there," Marcus observed, "why do you like them? Is there anything they all have in common that drew you to them?"

"I like a book that makes me think. Not always, sometimes I just want to put my mind into neutral and enjoy an easy read. Something along the lines of a comic, maybe. Calvin and Hobbes, Asterix, Far Side" – I was speaking at great length here – "But most of my favourite books are the ones that make me sit back and think 'fuck' once I've read them. The ones that stick with me."

When I studied Advanced Higher English in my final year of high school, I wrote a piece entitled, *Science vs. Free Will: an analogy of Anthony Burgess's 'A Clockwork Orange', 'Daniel Keyes' and 'Flowers for Algernon'*. I think I was the only student who actually enjoyed writing their final dissertation.

Again, I did not like talking about that stuff aloud. Or, at least not often. It made me sound incredibly pretentious. I only really spoke about reading and my opinions on novels with my mum; an equally passionate bookworm. Although Marcus probably couldn't tell that right now, as I wasn't shutting up. But hey, he was the one that gave me the chance to speak about a topic close to my heart.

"I'm sorta struggling now." I laughed nervously, trying to think of a fourth point. "I like that I'm vegetarian. It means a lot to me. I don't talk about it a lot because it makes me sound preachy, but I'm proud of it. Helping the animals, and shit."

Marcus smiled and waved his hand as if to say "Go on".

"If I was listening to someone else talk like this, I would think they were pretentious as fuck." I half-smiled.

"Well, I'm listening, and I don't think you are, so carry on."

"I think I'm good at giving presents. I like to put a lot of thought into it and make something meaningful. I made my friend Gaby a personalised board game for her birthday, and all the questions were about her. And Jake, my boyfriend, I made him a scrapbook on our anniversary."

"A board game?" Marcus looked impressed.

"Yeah." I smiled.

Ben and Gaby's birthdays were two days apart and we typically hosted a joint party for them. Their most recent birthday, late November last year, was their 21st.

I spent weeks on my presents for them. For Ben, I printed a top that had a picture of my face on it, and the words, *Heather is my best friend and my hero* on it, as a joke. And for Gaby, of course, I made a board game.

I took an old Cluedo game from the depths of my wardrobe. It had missing pieces and was of no use to anyone anymore. I painted over the board, before drawing squares around the edges, making a path for the players to follow. Each square had a different instruction on it, such as 'Take a shot!' or 'Take three drinks!' and 'Miss a turn!'.

One of the options was 'Take a card!'. For this, I had two piles. One pile were questions for Gaby and one pile were questions for the Struggle. Gaby's questions were trivia about us (such as 'How many siblings does Sam have?', which was three.) and similarly, our cards were about Gaby (for example, 'What is Gaby's favourite book?', which was The Handmaid's Tale.).

I also created counters for all of us; with each of our faces on them. I explained this to Marcus proudly.

"So, what you're telling me is you like something relating to your appearance, talent, education, morals and personality." Marcus looked triumphantly at his analysis of my list.

"Well, when you put it that way," I replied slowly. I understood the point he was trying to make, but I couldn't buy into it. I mean, he was being paid to make me feel better, he wasn't going to turn around and say anything negative about me.

"Okay, Heather, I think we've discussed some good things today. Unfortunately, there is nothing I can do in terms of helping you when you get home. So what you're going to need to do for me is to meet with your GP or doctor when you get home. Your nurse can write a letter for you to pass on to them, explaining what happened. You'll get put on a wait list of therapy, and see if they can make any changes toward your medication."

I nodded. "Okay, I can do that."

Marcus paused before saying, "Out of curiosity, what antidepressants are you currently on?"

"Sertraline."

Marcus frowned. "Sometimes, in very rare cases, antidepressants can increase suicidal thoughts."

"Of course it can," I groaned, feeling slightly more defeated than I already did.

"Right, anyway." Marcus stood up. "It was great meeting you, Heather, I hope you feel better."

He shook my hand, I thanked him and with that, he left. I watched as the curtains swung slightly then settled, trying to process the past half an hour.

I picked up my phone and, as expected, a surge of text messages had come through in the past few minutes, as more and more people began to find out about my situation.

ALISTAIR: *Hi, Heather! Hope you're feeling better! We will miss you this week.*

CONNOR: *Hi, Heather. I just found out what happened this week, and I hope you're okay. Although we all rip into each other at college we are the class of 2017! We are all here for you. Our strength is our friendship and we are the strongest group of friends I've ever known. I completely feel we have each other's backs through thick and thin. You're a great person, lass, and we all wish you a speedy recovery.*

GRAHAM: *Well, Heather. I heard the news. I hope you're okay. Are you still in the hospital?*

KAI: *Mate, I'm always here if you need me, okay? Seriously. I don't know how much this means to you, but I will be praying for you.*

The only person who hadn't been in touch with me yet was Ethan, who was with Kai, so would likely know by now.

The messages were moving, with no invasive questions, and just a lot of love. Even so, I had a sense that no one was entirely sure what to say to me. I couldn't blame them, I wouldn't know what to say if I was in their position. In fact, I don't know what to say to anyone right now even in my current position. At least we were all in the same boat; no one knew what to say to anyone.

I spent some time replying. It was just general thanks, copy and paste to each of them. I had run out of ways to respond to people.

I jumped slightly when my curtains were pulled back yet again. I was beginning to wonder why I had even bothered to pull them over and seclude myself; clearly, privacy was not a commonly practised exercise here.

I was mildly surprised at my next guest; it was Dr Thorne, the prick I hadn't seen since yesterday morning. He was examining his clipboard, full of notes about yours truly.

"How are you feeling today, Heather?" he asked, without even glancing up at me.

"Yeah, I'm fine." I got a murmur of acknowledgement in return, but I doubt he had even heard me.

"Right, well, we've got all your results back, and everything seems to be fine, so we can get you discharged now."

I raised my eyebrow. "Oh! Okay!"

"We'll get a nurse around soon to unhook you from the IV, and to take off the heart monitor," he said conclusively, before flattering me with some actual eye contact.

"You take care of yourself, okay? It was nice meeting you." He offered his hand to me, and I thanked him as I shook it.

My tests were clear! That was good news. I hadn't irreparably damaged my body – despite my attempt to do so. I had no clue what tests he was talking about – all I remembered was my heart monitor and the blood tests. But no one had really explained what they were for anyway. I suppose that was irrelevant now, considering there were no issues.

I sent a copied and pasted text to the people who most needed to know I was getting out; my parents, Jake, Leigh and Jamie, a bit of the old, *Hey! Guess what! Didn't ruin my body forever.*

By the time I had funnelled through all the predicted responses and sent back generic replies, Beth had swung back my curtain and appeared.

"Right." She beamed. "You'll be desperate to get all this stuff off you!"

"Fuck, yeah." I laughed.

She began by unscrewing the tube from my IV drip. The current bag still had about a third of its fluids left in it, but at least I wouldn't be needing that anymore. The machine began to beep furiously, protesting the disconnection, but Beth turned it off.

"I'm looking forward to not peeing every ten minutes," I said, relieved.

"That'll still last for a day or two, as it leaves your system," Beth confessed, and I groaned lowly.

Finally, she pulled the tube out of the nook of my arm. It felt much akin to a needle being pulled out after a blood test. I bent my right arm for the first time in days, feeling euphoric. Never again would I underestimate the joy of being able to move my arm completely.

Beth repeated the process on my left arm, with the redundant IV, and I couldn't help but shake my arms out with joy. After finally getting to bend my arms, I never wanted to extend them again. I would seriously consider a life as a T-Rex lady at this point.

Beth laughed when she was my physical relief. "Does that feel better?"

"So fucking much!"

"You're welcome to just peel off the heart monitor stuff yourself, and dump it all at the end of the bed," she said, her back to me as she tidied up the IV drip.

I slowly pulled at each of the small plasters, feeling them pull my skin up with it, wincing at the sharp pain. I reached down to my hospital gown, pulling the ones off my chest, before gathering the mess of wires onto my stomach. I took the monitor off from around my neck and stuck everything onto the end of my bed. I could, finally, move completely comfortably.

"So now, it's just a case of organising your release forms and you can head off!"

I paused. Thought for a moment, then said, "How am I getting back to my hotel?"

"Hm?" Beth raised her eyebrow at me.

"I came here by ambulance. I'm not even totally sure where I am. I certainly have no idea how to get back." I could feel a rising panic in my chest. I was quick to startle these days.

"I see. Let me see what I can do for you, whilst you get dressed."

I nodded complacently, as Beth disappeared. I didn't know how long she would be, so I didn't think twice about looking at my body as I dressed. I wanted to examine myself properly, naked, but now wasn't the time.

I threw off the clammy hospital gowns, covered in sweat and the odd drop of blood, and pulled on what I had been wearing two days ago when I was brought in.

I could feel the dried blood from Friday, hardened on my trousers, and pressing against my thighs. I shuddered.

I was fully dressed and packing up my belongings that Olivia and Ruaridh had dropped off yesterday before Beth returned.

"Okay!" she announced her presence with a celebratory clap, giving me a fright.

"We've booked a taxi for you. The hospital is paying for it, you don't need to worry about anything."

"Oh wow, really? Are you sure? That makes me feel so much better."

I was floored. How expensive was that going to be? I couldn't even remember how long my journey here had been; it was all a bit of a fog. Although, I suppose when you are being carted off to the hospital, you would not be concentrating on the time.

"They told us it would be about ten minutes, so you can come sit in the corridor until it arrives," Beth offered. It didn't sound like I had much of a choice, but I didn't mind. The nurses probably wanted to wipe down the bed and wheel in someone else to take my place.

Clutching my stuff, I turned my head to give one last look at the ward before I left. It was quiet, filled only with the noises of machines beeping, and someone turning in their bed. I didn't have long to take the view in, as Beth was walking away, leading me to my exit.

Bye, bye, Medical Assessment Unit.

I was brought to the ward I had sat in for hours on Friday night, squashed up in a wheelchair. I heard suitcase wheels rolling along the floor that I had vomited onto. It was certainly calmer than it had been when I was a guest here. It wasn't empty – there were still some people sitting about waiting, pained – but it wasn't as flooded as it had been. It must have been a welcome change for the nursing staff.

Beth took me to the main entrance of the A&E department, showing me where to sit. It was just some plastic blue seats, loosely held together by a metal beam underneath to create the idea of a bench. It was like it had been lifted straight from a bus stop.

"The driver knows to come to the entrance and ask for you, and everything has been paid for in advance," Beth informed me. I couldn't help but wonder if she had paid for it out of her own pocket. She seemed nice enough to have done so.

"Okay, thank you for everything," I wasn't sure what else to say. *Thank you for saving my life? For speaking to my dad? For helping me get back to my hotel?*

I'm sure she knew all the weight and meaning behind my words anyway, she had to.

Beth suddenly wrapped her arms around me, giving me a hug. She smelled of thick cleanliness, like bleach, and it made my eyes sting somewhat.

"You look after yourself, Heather, okay?" she said, standing back and looking at me seriously.

"Yeah, of course, I will."

I wasn't sure how much sincerity was behind my words. Beth nodded and turned and walked off, striding away to save more lives.

I had barely been able to sit on the hard plastic of the seats before a middle-aged man appeared at the entrance, looking around. He seemed to embody every physical stereotype a taxi driver was capable of having.

"Thompson?" he announced as if he were taking roll call.

"Yeah, hi, that's me." I stumbled to my feet, trying to grab everything at once. He came over and joined me, grabbing my suitcase, allowing me to grab the rest of my stuff and pull myself together.

I followed him outside, briefly feeling the air against my face properly for the first time in days. It was immediately refreshing.

He opened the boot of his car, and put my suitcase in a bit more roughly than I appreciated, as I opened the bag door and sat in my seat. I didn't know what type of car it was, but it was black and the leather seats were so smooth, I worried that I would slide off onto the floor, where I had put the rest of my stuff.

The driver made his way into the front seat, buckled himself in, fiddled with the Satnav, and pulled out.

"Did you see the game on Saturday?" he asked, turning his head to the right to watch his blind spot as we turned around a roundabout. The classic taxi-driver small talk topic.

"Football? Nah, I'm not a fan," I said, "I played rugby in high school, though. Only sport I ever managed to get into."

I saw his eyebrows raise in the mirror. "Oh yeah? Full contact or tag rugby?"

"Full contact. I was in the girl's team."

I had briefly decided to attempt the 'Duke of Edinburgh' scheme in school. I decided to join the newly born girl's rugby team, in order to tick off the 'physical' requirement.

Of course, I gave up doing the Duke of Edinburgh scheme. Rather quickly. However, much like my brass band, there was something about rugby that was gratifying enough to continue with. Perhaps the physical pain of being pummelled into the ground satisfied my need to hurt. Or perhaps it was when, about four months into it, I became the Captain of the team, and that made me feel incredibly validated. Regardless, there was something about walking home, covered head-to-toe in mud that made me feel like I had achieved something.

We were not a good team, by any means. None of us really cared much, however. Like myself, I think my teammates were just there in search of something fulfilling. In fact, we only had enough members to make the bare minimum required for an U18 team. All the school's attention was funnelled into the well-established and long-running boy's team, to the extent where our coach stopped coming to our bi-weekly practice in favour of going to the boy teams.

It was that passiveness from the P.E department that led me, and another teammate, Alice, to step into the captain and vice-captain roles. We led practice, rain or shine, instructing our teammates to tackle each other, yelling at them to remember their cheek should align with their rear end (a technique entitled 'cheek to cheek').

"What position?" the driver asked.

"Scrum-half."

I was a deceptively fast runner at the time. Which likely wouldn't be the case anymore as I settled into my laziness and gluttony, and tackling a flight of stairs usually took it out of me. But back then, when I was skinny and active, I could sprint at a pretty impressive rate, and take a tackle without much complaint.

"Not bad. I used to kick the ball around when I was in school, you know, afternoon kickabouts with your mates, but now I just watch it with a drink in hand." The driver laughed, and I offered him a polite chuckle, even though I wasn't remotely in the mood for small talk.

When I made no attempt to continue the conversation, my driver continued, "So how come you were in the hospital?"

"Oh, I have epilepsy, I've been having a lot of seizures," I lied. Who the hell asks that? And what if I had told him the truth?

Ah yes, Mr Taxi Driver stranger, I was in the hospital for a gory and brutal suicide attempt that, as you can see, failed. Take this next right, please!

Asshole.

"Ah, so they were just keeping an eye on you?" he poked further.

"Yeah, something like that."

I hoped my vague answer, paired with intensely staring out the window, would give him the hint that I didn't want to spend the next however many minutes dribbling out innate small talk.

It did not.

"Are you doing anything nice next weekend?" he asked, in that manner where he doesn't care about your answer, but he wants you to ask him.

"No, think I'll just take it easy." I sighed before asking. "You?"

"Going to the pub to watch the match with my mates, aye, it'll be good. I watched the last one in my house, but there is just something about the pub atmosphere that makes it that much better."

"I can imagine, yeah."

I don't really think he heard me before he continued talking.

"Aye, so going with my colleagues. Mikey will be a riot, he always is, swearing and getting drunk, arguing with fans of the opposite team. Hilarious."

It did not sound hilarious. Mikey sounded like a dick. The driver continued.

"Then we have a BBQ on Sunday, with the family. Aye, it'll be good. The wife, the kids, the in-laws. I'll be cooking, obviously."

Obviously.

"What are you planning on cooking?" I asked.

"Oh, the usual. Burgers, sausages, that sort of thing, you know?"

I did know.

"And, of course, beer."

Of course.

"What do you drink?"

"Oh, I'm more of a spirits sort of person, vodka, gin, rum," I responded, half-heartedly.

"Oh no, I never bother with that stuff. Especially those fruity cocktails, with the umbrella and shit."

"Oh, I love them, yeah."

"Nah, gotta go with beer or lager. Maybe a whiskey on a special occasion."

This driver felt like the other side of the coin, in comparison to Dr Thorne. One never shut up about useless drivel, and one only spoke about the bare minimum. I was slowly starting to miss Dr Thorne.

The drive had been about twenty minutes thus far, but I wasn't too sure how long it would take. Maybe ten more minutes? I tried to think back to the ambulance ride, but I wasn't concentrating too much on the journey's length at that point, for obvious reasons.

I didn't recognise the scenery either, but, there had been no windows in the back of the ambulance, so it was all new to me, regardless.

The last leg of the journey was equally tedious. I tuned out to most of it, just throwing in an occasional acknowledgement to the driver, who may have not even noticed.

Finally, I saw the comforting familiarity of where I had just spent the last week. The trees that bent over and brushed against the ground, the river running peacefully through the town and the new-born cygnets swimming clumsily.

We drove over the bridge that I had stood and phoned my grandparents on, which seemed like a lifetime ago. This entire weekend felt timeless; like a month of Sunday afternoons.

The driver pulled up slowly. I automatically reached for my purse to pay, before I realised that the hospital had sorted that out.

"Right, you look after yourself," the driver told me, as I grabbed my belongings desperately.

"Thank you, hope that weekend ends up being good," I said politely, smiling, as I left the car.

I walked through the courtyard to the entrance of our usual hotel, the one my fellow students and I stayed in when studying, not the one I had attempted in.

The courtyard was pleasant, especially in the summer. There were wooden benches, with tables, to sit at and maybe nurse a drink (why did everything I do involve a drink?). There was an elegant water feature, almost like a fountain, with water coming out the top of a large metal orb, and pouring down the sides of it, over and over. It was indescribably relaxing.

I pushed open the front doors, smacking my suitcase against it as I stumbled through. The receptionist was watching me, probably internally laughing at my complete incompetence. I approached the desk and noticed that this receptionist was new. Well, maybe new, or I just haven't met her before. She was young, perhaps a couple years older than me, and admittedly very stunning, with long auburn hair going past her shoulders. I knew Ruaridh would be pleased to check in later, she was his type.

I checked in, although I'd only be there for the night. She gave me my hotel key, room 75, and I sauntered off to find it.

By the time I reached my room, I was sticking to myself with sweat again. Heaving a suitcase up three flights of stairs on an unforgivingly warm afternoon was quite the task.

The room was simple and understated, but certainly more attractive than the hotel I found myself in on Friday. I had two single beds, with a bedside cabinet in between. A large, wooden wardrobe sat in one corner of the room, with a matching desk in the other corner. An old television that still had a VHS slot sat on the desk. I wasn't going to get much use from that.

I dumped my suitcase on one of the beds and texted Jake to let him know I was back in the hotel. It was around 5 pm.

Jamie was going to be another half an hour, give or take, and my dad would not be here until 9 pm easily.

I ran my hand through my hair, feeling how disgusting it was, a gross combination of sweat, lack of brushing and three days in the hospital. I needed a shower, and soon, before anyone else began arriving. I dug out some fresh clothes from my suitcase and wandered into the bathroom, shutting the door behind me, even though no one was there.

I stripped and was just about to get into the shower when I realised something. My bandages. I couldn't get them wet, so I'd have to take them off. Thankfully Beth had given me some fresh ones when I was back in the hospital, for this exact purpose.

I sat on the toilet seat and slowly undid the knot on my right arm. I pulled it, and the bandage began to give way. I unwrapped it a few times before the whole length of it fell onto the floor. Still sticking to my arm was some dressing, which I steadily pulled off. It stung and I inhaled sharply through my teeth. It had stuck to my healing cuts, and I had to prise it with some light force. It was opening a couple of the gashes again, and a few drops of blood ran down my arm. I repeated the process with my left arm.

I studied my lower arms for a moment. This was the first time I had seen them since getting my stitches on Friday. The edges of the stitching on my right arm were an angry red; fighting against my skin to pull the flesh together. A monstrous bruise ran down the entirety of my right forearm; yellow, black, purple and green. The colours of the world's most melancholy rainbow. I wasn't too sure what had caused this; whether it was the violence of my own actions or the result of the several local anaesthetic injections.

The butterfly stitching on my left arm was curling a little at the ends, and small bits of fluff were sticking to the exposed adhesive.

I stood and climbed into the bath. There was a shower attachment above it, which was the quicker option out of the two. I turned the shower on, and the full force of a stream of cold water hit me in the face. I shuddered but didn't step back. As the water bounced off my arm and legs, I felt a violent sting. I was careful not to go against the advice of the hospital staff and soak my arms, just letting the coolness bounce off them for a few seconds, before sticking my face directly into the water stream.

I must have lost track of the time because I heard my phone vibrating continuously from where it sat on the sink, and I snapped out of my daydream. I turned the shower off, wrapped a towel around myself, and clambered out of the bath.

I had just missed a phone call from Jamie. It was 5.40 pm. As I went to phone him back, a text came through.

JAMIE: *That's me here. What room are you in? I'll keep you company until your dad gets here.*

HEATHER: *Room 75. Give it 10 minutes, I'm just out of the shower.*

Jamie sent back a thumbs up.

I quickly dried myself, stuck some new clothes on, and attempted to redress my arms, before realising I couldn't do it one-handed. I swore to myself as I tried to wrap it around without it becoming loose at the other end, but it was a futile effort. Yet again, I was going to ask too much from Jamie and get his assistance.

Almost as if he felt his ears burning, Jamie knocked on my door. I grabbed a cardigan, not particularly wanting to greet him with my arms on show. I pulled the door open.

"Hi," I said, breathlessly, as if I had been running.

"Come here," Jamie said fondly, gesturing for me to hug him. I did. It felt surreal to see him in person, after everything that had happened the past few days. It seemed like an eternity since I had last seen him, and everything had changed between us now. All that in the space of a few days.

"You're gonna make me greet again." I laughed, pulling back. Did they use the term 'greet' in England, or was that Scottish-only slang?

"How are you?" Jamie asked, coming in and sitting on the single bed that hadn't been taken over by my suitcase.

"I'm fine. I mean, I'm not, but I'm fine."

"I think that's the best thing we can hope for right now." Jamie smiled at me.

"I'm pushing my luck here, and you can say no, but I need help with something." I tried to sound as casual as I could, acutely aware of the risk of putting pressure on him.

Jamie raised an eyebrow. "What is it?"

"I had to take my bandages off before I showered, and I can't get the new ones on one-handed, could you help me?"

"Oh, yeah, no worries." Jamie was completely unfazed by my request.

"Are you sure? My arms look fucking grim."

"Honestly, let me help you because otherwise it'll hurt and get infected."

"Right okay, yeah." I nodded, digging out the fresh bandages and dressed Beth had passed onto me. There were only two, one for each arm. I'd have to buy more when I got

149

home. I passed them to Jamie, who began peeling the plastic off. I slid my cardigan off my shoulders and put it down softly behind me.

Jamie stood up, at eye level with me. He wrapped his hand around my wrists, turning my arms so he could see them clearly. He examined them for a moment, before finally saying, "They're so deep, Heather."

"Yeah," I said quietly. There was a moment of silence between us.

"Right," Jamie said purposefully, breaking the silence, "let me sort this out."

I stuck my right arm out and watched as he put the dressing on my forearm gingerly.

"Hold that down for me for a second," he instructed. I pressed down. It hurt.

He grabbed the bandage and began wrapping it around. A silence had fallen between us, but it wasn't uncomfortable. In fact, this was perhaps the most settled I felt all weekend. Jamie was easy to talk to, and should I want it, the conversation would flow. Nonetheless, I felt no pressure to talk. All weekend I had been juggling plenty of conversations; medical teams asking how I felt, friends and family texting wanting constant updates, making arrangements for this, that and the next thing. For once, I had the company with none of the badgerings to share how I felt.

Jamie finished my left arm and took a step back to admire his handy work. He nodded as if to say "Yup, good job".

"Hey, not bad," I said, twisting my arm around to look at it. The ends of the bandages had been tied together in a small knot in the middle of each arm, before being tucked in to avoid it coming loose.

"I should be a nurse." Jamie grinned, as he sat back down on the bed.

Just then, I heard my phone go off. It was Ethan.

ETHAN: *Kai and I just got to the hotel. She's away to shower and sort herself out, unpack and stuff. Are you here? Do you need some company? Can come to my room if you want.*

HEATHER: *Hey, yeah I'm here. I'm in my room with Jamie, if you don't mind him coming too?*

ETHAN: *Actually, I'd rather you just send Jamie and you stayed in your room.*

Ethan added a winking emoji, complete with its tongue sticking out. He was obviously joking, and I was appreciative of what he was doing. Bar Jamie, and Jake, no one else had been particularly normal, for lack of a better term. As if they were scared that a joke would set me off, and I would wind up in the hospital again. Screw that. I need humour, I need a reason to laugh and smirk, and to get that brief flush of positivity.

Ethan and I always made fun of each other, and he knew us, and our friendship, well enough to not wrap me in cotton wool and be excessively considerate.

I returned the favour with some light teasing.

HEATHER: *That's fair, I think seeing you would make me feel worse, to be honest. What room are you in, so I can send Jamie?*

ETHAN: *It'd make anyone feel worse, let's be real. And room twenty-three.*

"Fancy taking this pity party to Ethan's? He's offered to let us hang out in his room," I suggested to Jamie.

"Sure." He shrugged.

I grabbed my key card and my phone. Just as we were about to leave, I turned, grabbing my cardigan and hurriedly pulling it over me. I doubted Ethan would want to see my arms, despite the expert bandaging done by Jamie.

When Ethan opened the door to Jamie and I's smiling faces, he let Jamie in before jokingly shutting the door in my face and saying, "Nope, you're not getting in, piss off." I laughed wildly and could have hugged him from how grateful I was for his efforts to make sure nothing was different between us.

There was no "How are you?" with the patronising, high-pitched voice, and the head tilt. No questions about my hospital stay, or awkwardness over not knowing what to say. There was just a room, with two friends, who were offering a momentary distraction.

Ethan's room was notably different from mine. He was armed with a double bed, and a bunk bed, which took me by surprise. The room, as a result, was considerably wider than mine too. His window overlooked the car park, however, which wasn't the most memorable of views.

"I'm ill, I get to lie on the double bed," I declared, tossing my phone and key card onto the bedside table and claiming the left side of the bed. Ethan sat next to me, and Jamie pulled up an armchair. He sat down, and propped his legs onto the bed, just below where I had crossed mine into a basket.

As Jamie and Ethan chatted, I took the chance to give Jake an update.

HEATHER: *Jamie came into my room to see me. He gave me a huge hug and helped me put new bandages on after my shower. There was a moment where he just stared at my arms and told me how deep my cuts were.*

JAKE: *He's so nice. He is being so brilliant.*

HEATHER: *Ethan invited us to hang out in his room, so we are just chilling here for now. He's being really nice, because he's treating me totally normally, like doing friendly teasing and stuff. It's a welcome break from everyone asking how I am.*

JAKE: *I bet, babe. Want me to bully you too? Would that cheer you up?*

I smiled down at my phone when I read his text.

"When is everyone else getting in?"

I looked up at Jamie, who had just asked. Ethan frowned, thinking.

"Kai is already here, she's just in her room at the moment. Graham is flying in from Ireland, so I don't actually know when he will be here. Olivia is only an hour away. I think Ruaridh is on his way in, so again, maybe an hour or so. I think Alistair is driving in with him, actually, I don't remember. I have no idea about Connor," he concluded.

I nodded. "Seems accurate enough. I haven't eaten in days, I'm gonna need food before I go" – I was just thinking out loud at this point – "I think I'll just order in."

"Yeah, let's do that," Jamie agreed.

"Oh, don't feel you have to order in just because I am," I said hurriedly, "it's just cause I'm not up to going out."

"Well yeah, we'll keep you company," Jamie retorted.

"That makes me feel bad!" I pleaded.

"Well, don't."

"There we go, you've solved all my problems." I rolled my eyes.

"I'm down to order," Ethan added, "I'll text people and see who is coming soon, we can order for them."

153

"But what if they want to go out?" I was being annoying, and I knew that, but I just hated the thought of people changing their schedules to suit me.

"Then they can go out, but we want to keep you company," Jamie said firmly.

"Okay." I sighed, defeated.

Ethan let out a surprised "Oh!" and I turned to face him, looking quizzical.

"So Ruaridh and Alistair are only about half an hour away, Alistair says they're down, they want to know what we are getting. Kai says she's down too, she'll come join us when the food arrives," he explained.

Jamie and Ethan looked at me expectedly.

"So I need to decide this too?" I said, exacerbated.

"I don't like this pressure."

"Well, the one who nearly died gets to choose what we order." Ethan grinned at me as I tried, and failed, to hide a smile at his morbid joke.

"Fine, I want pizza," I conceded.

"Fair enough." If Ethan had a catchphrase, it would have been that. His thumbs tapped hurriedly against his phone screen, updating the other two.

"We can order it on my phone, I'll pay, just transfer me the money." Jamie handed me his phone, with the app already opened.

"What a generous offer," I snorted.

My go-to order was always cheese pizza with jalapenos. If I could, I would have jalapenos on anything. In fact, I wouldn't be opposed to just sitting with a jar of jalapenos, and eating them like a packet of crisps.

Ethan had dug out a pack of cards from his bag. "Game of cards whilst we wait?"

By the time Ruaridh and Alistair had arrived, checked in, and dumped their suitcases, the pizza had arrived, and Kai had joined us. Alistair had sprawled out along the bottom of the double bed, which was increasingly running out of the room. Ruaridh was stretched across the lower bunk bed. Kai sat on the top bunk, looking down at us, probably feeling quite mighty.

I was worried about how Alistair and Kai would react to seeing me. Of course, Ruaridh was not phased; any awkwardness between us was conquered the day before in the hospital. Luckily, however, it was fine. Alistair had offered me a delicate hello, and Kai marched right around the bed to hug me.

The noise of people chewing and chatting fell into the background as I spoke to Jake. I was aching to see him. My friends were great, but I needed to be in the safety of my boyfriend's company. Although it was only a week, it felt like an age since I saw him last.

JAKE: *Has anyone said anything about you leaving soon?*

HEATHER: *No, we're just having pizza, and we're still in Ethan's room.*

JAKE: *That's nice, who's there?*

HEATHER: *Me, Ethan, Jamie, Alistair, Ruaridh and Kai.*

JAKE: *How are you feeling?*

HEATHER: *A bit shaky, actually.*

I sat my pizza box to the side. I had overestimated my ability to eat and only managed through two pieces before my stomach began churning. I frowned. I felt warm, too warm, and my hands were shaking. I felt a tight, uncomfortable sensation in my chest.

I had to get out of the room.

"I need to go for a minute," I said suddenly, before I stood up, grabbing my things, abandoning my pizza, and darting out the room.

I sped up the stairs, my anxiety inflating with each step I took. It took me two tries before I could unlock my door; my hands were trembling too much to keep steady.

I flew into the bathroom, the door barely shutting behind me. Dropping onto my knees, I stuck my head into the toilet and heaved violently, feeling my entire body ache. Whatever small amount of food I had managed to force down was certainly coming up now.

I flushed the toilet, and sat back, wiping my mouth off the back of my hand. My entire body was quivering; I was exhausted. And the last thing I wanted was to have to handle being sick.

I pulled myself up, and staggered back into my bedroom, collapsing onto my bed. My stomach had eased, but not entirely.

My eyes began watering. I was burning up, feeling entirely too uncomfortable, with a pounding chest. I was lying on my back, and I felt the coolness of my tears running down the sides of my face.

The vibrating of my phone at the end of the bed interrupted my panic attack.

JAMIE: *Are you okay, mate?*

HEATHER: *I felt really unwell and overwhelmed. Went to my room to throw up and cry.*

JAMIE: *Want me to come up?*

HEATHER: *Yeah, treat yourself, come see me crying in person instead of hearing it over the phone.*

The sound of a light chap filled my room a couple of minutes later. I opened the door, greeting my continually selfless friend with a puffy, red, tear-stained face.

I turned around, not even offering a greeting, and lay back down, staring at the ceiling. Jamie dropped himself onto my other bed.

I couldn't stop shivering. My breathing was equally unsteady, combined with the nasal sound of my whimpering.

"Here" – Jamie stuck his arm out – "take my hand."

"What?" I sniffed.

"I'm serious. You're shaking. Take my hand."

I did. His hand was cool, welcomingly cool, especially in comparison to the hot flash I was having. It wasn't until he had wrapped his fingers around me that I noticed how intensely my hand was trembling. Jamie's hand was steady and unmoving. I felt marginally eased.

"Want a distraction?" Jamie offered. I nodded.

"Okay." Jamie thought momentarily. "What was that worst shag you've ever had?"

The question was so unexpected, that I snorted with laughter, coughing a little, "Really?"

"I'm serious." Jamie chuckled. "What was the absolute worst shag you've ever had?"

"Well, not Jake, obviously," I began.

"Obviously."

I thought about it for a moment, before smiling. I looked up at the ceiling in embarrassment, not wanting to meet his eyes. "I think I have the answer."

"Let's hear it then."

I let go of his hand, and sat up, crossing my legs into a basket. "This is awful, please don't judge me, it was not my fault" – I held my hand up – "And I promise I'm better than this."

"Uh oh."

"I had a one-night stand with this guy, and it was like sleeping with a corpse."

"What?" Jamie stared at me.

"Oh yeah. He didn't touch me once, at all. I'm not even kidding."

"How does that even work?" Jamie looked, understandably, very confused.

"I walked into the room, he was already naked! So I'm on my knees just going to town on his dick, and he doesn't make a single noise. At all."

"How can you not make a noise?"

"I don't know!" I exclaimed.

"I'm not that bad! Then after a bit he just looked at me and said, '*Do you want to sit on it*?'"

"How romantic," Jamie snorted sarcastically.

"So we go to bed, and I'm riding his dick like there is no tomorrow, and then," I groaned as I thought back to this, "he still made no noise. And didn't touch me once, didn't even kiss me."

"That's awful, that is truly awful." Jamie looked disgusted; making me laugh even more.

"I am so glad I have Jake now."

"No wonder." Jamie rolled his eyes.

"Haven't you been talking to a girl recently?" I remembered suddenly.

"Not to imply that the memory of the worse sex I've had to date makes me think of your love life."

"Yeah." Jamie smiled. "Chloe. I met her at my job. She's great."

"Are you official yet?" I smirked.

"Nah, it's only been a few weeks."

"Let me see her!"

Jamie pulled out his phone and scrolled through a couple photos before settling on one. He passed it to me, looking a bit proud of himself. Chloe was incredibly pretty. She was dainty, with gorgeous eyes, and a glowing smile. Her hair was a soft, sandy blonde that sat at shoulder length.

"Well, I'll definitely be stealing her from you." I grinned.

"Good luck with that one, because now I know you're crap in bed."

My phone buzzed gently next to me. It was Ethan.

ETHAN: *Can we come join you in your room?*

HEATHER: *Yeah, I feel better. Room 75.*

"We're being joined by the others again," I told Jamie.

"Why are they coming here? Your room is tiny, we should be going back to them."

"I'm not fucking moving." I laughed, as Jamie sighed at my endearing laziness, even though we both knew I genuinely didn't have the strength to move.

It was only a couple of minutes before my door was banging. Jamie stood, and opened the door slightly, before saying, "Password?"

I heard Ethan telling him, "Fuck off", and Jamie saying, "Correct", before swinging the door to let them in.

Ethan, Alistair, Ruaridh and Kai poured into my room, but they were joined by others. Olivia, Connor and Graham had arrived too and crept into my room behind them. Everyone was here to see me off.

Connor and Graham looked a little uncertain, as they hadn't seen me yet. But I think my smiling face, and the fact that everyone else seemed comfortable enough, allowed them to relax a bit.

"When did you get here?" I directed my question at the newcomers.

"We all sort of just turned up at the lobby at the same time." Olivia laughed. "We heard the party was getting held here."

"Some party," I snorted.

"We brought your pizza up." Ruaridh handed it to me, I nodded at him in thanks but knew I wasn't going to be touching it.

Everyone settled down as best as they could, in a room with two single beds and two armchairs. Jamie and I sat at the top of each bed, Ruaridh and Graham laid claim to the two armchairs before anyone else could, Kai and Ethan squeezed up in my bed, Alistair joined Jamie on his bed, and Olivia stood in the doorway of the bathroom, watching us all.

I found myself hoping Olivia wouldn't be able to tell I had vomited recently in said bathroom.

We looked like a bunch of ten-year-olds at a sleepover, about to talk about boys they liked and make prank phone calls. Which would've probably been quite fun.

That passing thought triggered a memory I had forgotten about until now. Years ago, when I was around thirteen, I was on the receiving end of a prank phone call. I couldn't remember exactly what was said, I think they were claiming to be a bloke called Gary from a gas company.

I just remember finding out a few hours later that it has been Ryan who was behind it, and some friend of his I had never met called Jake.

The world is a small, and funny place.

"Are you staying the week then or going home?" Graham asked me. A sort of silence fell across the room, someone had dared ask a question that loosely hinted at what I had done. I didn't mind. Elephants in the room stop being elephants when you pluck up the courage to actually talk about it. I inwardly guffawed at my attempt to seem philosophical. Even my internal monologue was sick of me.

"Yeah, my dad is on his way to grab me right now, actually." I smiled.

"Driving? How long is that going to take?" Connor raised his eyebrows.

"Six hours both ways."

"Fucking hell, are you going to stay the night then, like?" Alistair chimed in.

"No, just want to get home as soon as possible, to be honest, so I'll get in around three."

"What time is it right now, then?"

"Um, it's about 7:50." Ethan checked his watch.

"You don't need to stay here and keep me company, go out or something," I said, desperate to let them know that this gathering was not something I was insisting had to happen.

"Heather, shut up," Kai said. That was that. I mimicked zipping my lips shut, and throwing away the key.

"Now if only we could make that permanent," Ethan joked.

"Man, you really need to get some more original banter." I rolled my eyes.

"You are not worthy of earning my good banter," Ethan retorted, smiling. I laughed and was grateful for it. A simple laugh can lift a lot of weight off your shoulders.

"I tell you what," Connor said suddenly, "I went to the loo with Graham before we came up, and he has a powerful hose."

The room erupted into laughter at this ridiculously unexpected statement.

"You did not just say that," Olivia said between furious giggles.

"What can I say?" Graham boasted.

"Looks like I have some competition," Ruaridh added, smirking lowly.

"No, stop, enough," Kai begged, "I don't want these images in my head."

"Does anyone?" Jamie groaned.

"I've had a bad enough weekend as is, and now this!"

A couple of faces in the room dropped suddenly at my attempt at a joke. I bit my inner cheek, realising that was probably a comment I should have kept to just Ethan and Jamie.

Olivia sensed the awkward fog that had spread in the room, and brightly said, "Heather, I've found a club where we could go to eventually, but I don't know if it'll cause you a seizure or not, because of the lights."

"Show her a video and if she hits the floor, she can't go," I heard Jamie suggest to my right.

More laughter.

"No, wait, wait, for real though." Ethan raised his hand to silence the room, before looking at me. "Do you use a vibrator or do you just use a dildo and a strobe light?"

"Better than that, Jake aims a strobe light at me when we have sex," I retaliated, sticking my tongue out.

"Let's be honest, it's dangerous for any of us to go into clubs." Connor pointed out. "We're idiots when we are drunk."

"You're not wrong," Jamie agreed, "we're absolute specimens."

"Do you remember," Alistair reminisced, "our first week here?"

"I think you mean the week Jamie sat on my debit card and snapped it in two with his ass," Ruaridh said, bitterly, but with a fondness in the voice at the memory from a year ago.

"I bought you a drink as an apology!" Jamie reminded him.

"That was also the week Alistair snapped my ring from Jake in two," I added, jogging everyone's memory.

"Oh my God, yeah!" Olivia exclaimed.

"I must have missed this, what happened?" Kai raised an eyebrow, and Alistair sank a little lower down, looking shameful, but laughing.

"We were in the pub nearby, the one with the weird bartender," I explained.

"The weird bartender that *you* added on Facebook." Ethan pointed out.

"Yes, well, that isn't relevant, I was drunk, leave me alone." I waved his comment away. "And Alistair wanted to try on this promise ring that Jake had given me, but his chubby fingers were too fat for it and he snapped it in two," I added, sarcastically, throwing a grin at him.

"Oi!" Alistair said, mockingly insulted.

The promise ring had been beautiful. It was £60, which, to two 17-year-olds in minimum wage jobs, was a huge spend. It was petite; a small, silver, beaded ring made to look like a tiara. Not what I would have chosen nowadays, but, at that point, it was stunning.

It wasn't an engagement ring, but it was a promise ring. It was like one of those daft, teenage, romantic films. The ones where the guy presents the girl with a promise ring, telling her that it is a vow to be there for her, a comment on their future together, and an assurance that one day, that ring will be upgraded to an engagement ring, then a wedding ring.

But to me, it wasn't daft. We were teenagers, and completely in love, but it was not daft.

I remember being tipsy when Alistair accidentally snapped it, and I began crying. But, of course, it was accidental, so I was quick to forgive him and his size-too-big fingers.

"Do you still have it?" Alistair queried.

"Actually yes, in two pieces in my jewellery box, I kept saying I'll get it fixed but never got around to it."

Maybe that was something I could do now that I have all this extra time on my hands.

"Was that the week Heather and Olivia got really drunk, and I had to help Olivia to her feet after she fell over?" Jamie wondered aloud.

"We are not talking about that." Olivia glared at him. "Never."

The room was full of positive energy I was longingly soaking up, with all the fond memories being shared, and everyone laughing and poking fun at each other.

"I'm pretty sure I still have a photo of you getting helped up," I teased.

"Delete it. Or I will kill you," Olivia threatened.

"No way, I'm keeping this forever, I can't get rid of quality content like that."

"You say that as if we don't have a million awful photos of you, Heather," Ruaridh's Welsh accent joined in on the conversation.

"You know, now that you mention it, we do have the photos of Heather ice-skating that year," Ethan said slowly, enjoying the look on my face as he brought up that horrifically embarrassing memory.

"This is harassment!" I claimed, watching everyone pull out their phones to dredge up some of my least flattering moments.

The infamous 'ice-skating' photos were taken during our last week together before Christmas last year. We had visited the local market, and it was beautiful. Rows of wooden stalls lined the city centre, covered in fairy lights, tinsel and baubles. Everything was illuminated, and beautiful. People were bustling about, dawning hats and scarfs, clutching churros or hot chocolate. It wasn't snowing, it rarely did, but the air was crisp and cool. And accompanied with Christmas music being played through speakers, it felt incredibly festive: the perfect way to start a holiday.

Then, of course, Olivia suggested we go ice-skating.

I used to ice-skate in the local indoor rink when I was young, and naively assumed that those skills would be transferable to a real, no-holds-barred, outdoor rink. I bragged myself up to everyone, about how I was a naturally good skater, and despite not having done it in ages, I would be absolutely fine and pick it back up no bother.

What happened next was certainly some karmic justice for my bragging.

Everyone had been skating, having a great time, whilst I slid about nervously against the walls, with all the under-five-year-olds. Jamie tried to encourage me to skate out to the middle, but I refused: the ice was significantly slippier than the man-made, indoor rinks I was used to.

Eventually, Connor skated over to me, linked arms with me, and told me he would stick with me whilst we went into the middle. This went as awfully as could be imagined.

I stumbled, whether due to overly enthusiastic skating as I put my trust into Connor or due to a higher being striking me down to keep me humble. I took Connor to the ground with me, and we both smacked against the solid ice below us. Connor managed to pull himself back up almost immediately, but I wasn't as lucky, or graceful.

I couldn't get back onto my feet, and like I was straight out of a Laurel and Hardy sketch, I just kept falling onto my ass over and over. Eventually, two staff members had to come and help me to my feet, each one grabbing one of my arms to hoist me up.

The cherry on top was that, not only did everyone watch, but they took photos too, documenting my complete inability to stand. The photos, capturing me attempting to pull myself up before being manhandled by staff members in high-visibility jackets, have made their rounds several times.

"As if I'm the only one of us who has acted like a twat." I defended myself, blushing at the memory, but giggling regardless.

"No, I'm sure it's just you," Kai concluded.

"I feel like I'm in court, trying to defend myself here," I snorted.

"Present your findings that prove that any of us are half as bad as you," Jamie challenged me.

I scrunched my face, examining everyone in the room, picking my victim to share a humiliating story on. I settled my gaze onto Ruaridh.

"What about the time he ate so much at a buffet that he immediately threw up the second we left the restaurant?" I pointed at him, accusing him in the court of idiots.

"That was grim, to be fair," Olivia grimaced, but Ruaridh proudly claimed he had no regrets.

I felt like I had had too much alone time with my thoughts this weekend. Texting ones doesn't deafen your internal monologue like conversation does. Lying in the hospital gave me too much space to dwell on my feelings, and Friday night was an internal debate all in itself. But right now, nothing was going through my mind. I was in this moment, with my colleagues, sharing stories of our less finer moments. Or rather, mainly *my* less finer moments. I wonder how long it would be before we could all sit and laugh about this one particularly low moment of my life. Perhaps never.

"Do any of you still have your presents from last Christmas?" Graham broke through my momentary thoughts.

"Of course I still do," I said, proudly.

"Well obviously you would, you got the best fucking one," Kai said, grievously.

"You're just complaining because you ended up with my gift," I retorted.

Last Christmas, the Christmas of my dramatic fall, we decided to opt-out of a college secret Santa gift exchange, and instead, we played 'Evil Santa'.

The idea was that each one of us would take turns to purchase a present; anything our imagination could think of. When we gathered for our last week of college before we broke for Christmas, we piled all the gifts onto a table. Sitting in a circle, we pulled names out of a hat to determine who went and when. When your name was pulled, you chose one of the gifts from the bundle and opened it.

At this point, if you didn't like the gift, you could swap it, but only with someone who had gone before you. This meant that the first person to pick a gift was forced to keep what they have, whilst the last person had free reign of everyone's presents. Luck had been on my side last year; I was the last person to go, and I used that power rather wickedly.

By the end of it, I was the one of only two people who had an acceptable gift. I had gained a personalised mug, with a quote from one of our lecturers, saying "I HATE COMPUTERS". This was particularly funny to us, as he taught IT. Jamie ended up with a glass-framed photo of us, from our first-ever day in college; the only sentimental gift amongst the lot.

The others, however, weren't quite so lucky. Ruaridh ended up with Donald Trump's biography, which got binned almost immediately. Connor received a rather haunting-looking Santa toilet seat cover, with dead, vacant eyes and I'm still not sure if he made use of it. Ethan, somewhat similarly, got an awfully painted nativity scene ornament, in which baby Jesus looked like he was melting. Alistair had gotten exactly three bunches of bananas, in a plastic bag; a result of

Graham's peculiar gift-giving. Graham himself came away with an onion wrapped in a picture of Shrek; a genius reference from Connor. Olivia got a giant, purple, rotating dildo from Ruaridh, whilst Kai got the best present of all: a t-shirt with my face on it.

"I'm still completely wounded that I've never seen you wear that wonderful t-shirt, Kai," I teased.

"I took it home, and melted it with bleach."

Alistair pulled a vague face, before saying, "I think I ended up giving all my bananas, and Graham's onion, to a homeless guy we walked past."

"I really hope he didn't eat the onion," Olivia grimaced.

"Speaking of eating" – Ruaridh bent forward, opened my pizza box I hadn't touched, and took a slice – "Thanks, Heather."

"Asshole."

There was a knock at the door, interrupting our conversation. I quickly glanced at my phone, it was just after 9 pm. But I feel that I could have figured out that it was my dad anyway, due to his distinctive, booming knock that only a father could have.

Ethan jumped up before anyone else could, and opened that door.

"Hello!" I said, quite enthusiastically, dragging out my 'o'. I was overjoyed to see a family member. Yes, I loved my friends who were squished into my room, but there was a comforting, life-long familiarity that my father brought into the room with him.

I pointed to each person in the room, introducing them to my dad. Everyone seemed overly polite; probably worrying

169

that he was going to bring up what happened in front of everyone. But I knew my dad, and he wouldn't do that to me.

"Yeah, I'm going to struggle to remember those names," he admitted. I probably should have warned him that people were gathered in my room.

We laughed.

"I only have one question," Graham said, a somewhat serious look on his face as he directed the question to my dad, "do you call them 'tidgy puds' too?"

"Absolutely," Dad said triumphantly, "that's the best terminology."

The room erupted into groans, with comments like "What?" and "No way!" being bounced around.

"Thank you." I waved my arm toward Dad, "this is the support I need."

Tidgy puds, was what my family called Yorkshire puddings. It just stuck over time, and I often forget that no one else refers to them as that. When I casually mention 'tidgy puds' during a conversation, I'm met with raised eyebrows and a great deal of confusion.

This wasn't the only peculiar thing I did when it came to speech or pronunciation. I was incapable of pronouncing words with 'th' in them – leather, weather, the, etc – and they came out with a definitive 'lur' sound. To explain further; instead of saying "leather" I would say "lealur". I always used my overbite as an excuse and would say that my tongue couldn't go between my teeth to make the proper sound. But, truthfully, I'm not sure why I do it. And, of course, there was the obvious cruel irony of my name being Heather. My mum would always say that, if she had known how I was going to speak, she would have named me something else.

This was hilarious for many people, and several times when my friends and I have a drink in us, they'll begin begging me to say certain words; laughing about it. I just hope they were laughing with me. On the rare occasions where I accidentally manage to say one of those words correctly, I'm met with praise, and it makes me feel like a child learning to talk.

Another problem word for me was 'idea', and in this case, I would add an unnecessary 'r' at the end, creating the word 'idear'. Something that was a pet peeve of Jake's, but something I couldn't help but do.

Bar the controversial 'tidgy puds', the somewhat funny 'th' problem and my boyfriend's bugbear, I spoke normally.

However, it didn't stop my mum from suggesting speech therapy. I always refused. Jokes on her too, because I was part of my high school's public speaking and debating team.

"You all packed?" My dad looked around the room for my suitcase.

"Aye," I said. Being in England always brought out more of my Scottishness as if I needed to reassure others and myself that I wasn't English.

I stood, grabbing my suitcase and passing it over the bed to my dad.

"How long did it take you to travel down?" Graham asked my dad. Even though I had already told everyone, I assumed it was just Graham's attempt to make conversation.

"About six hours, give our take." Dad pulled a face, trying to remember. "Yeah, six hours, I left at 3 pm."

Graham let out a low breath, impressed.

"So you won't get home until, like, 3 am?" Connor did the maths. Again, even though I had already told them this.

"Yup!" Dad seemed to be enjoying my cohort's admiration for his dedication to me. Although I don't think anyone was more touched than myself.

"Right, goodbye time, because I want to get home pronto." I pulled my handbag over my shoulder and clapped my hands together. I wasn't wholly in a rush but didn't want to make the goodbye process or small talk last longer than necessary.

I went around the room, hugging each of them one by one; Olivia, Jamie, Ethan, Alistair, Connor, Kai and Graham. When I reached Ruaridh, he offered me a formal handstand, and I accepted it, laughing.

A mild sentimental mood filled me, as I realised I wasn't sure when I would see them next. I would miss them that was an inarguable fact.

My dad opened the door and began walking to the hall. Suddenly something clicked, and I turned around, digging my room key card out of my pocket. I handed it to Jamie, who was closest to me.

"Can you check out for me?"

"Yeah, 'course."

I smiled at the group, offered one last goodbye, and then left to join my dad in the hallway, walking down the stairs to the front entrance, and leaving the hotel.

When we arrived at the car (which was mercifully parked close to the hotel) Dad popped open the boot, and put my suitcase in it for me. I opened the passenger side door, wondering if the group I left behind were watching from the window.

"So, I got you a pillow and a blanket, so you can be nice and comfy on the drive home," Dad explained when he noticed me staring at my seat.

"Thank you." I smiled. "That's brilliant." I threw my handbag onto the floor of the car.

"One thing before you go in."

I turned, facing my dad, slightly confused until he pulled me into a hug. Hugs from my dad were my favourite. It was exactly what I needed. He always said, 'it wasn't a real hug until your back cracked', meaning he always held you tightly.

"I love you," Dad reminded me.

"Thank you, I love you too."

He let go of me, and we climbed into the car. Just then, Jake texted me. I gave him an update.

JAKE: *How's it going?*

HEATHER: *Everyone refused to go out for dinner without me, so we had pizza. We sat in Ethan's room chatting, but I began to feel really ill. So I had to run back to my room. I ended up being sick and having a really bad panic attack. I was lying on my bed shaking really violently and cramping and crying. Jamie came up to keep me company and calmed me down. When I felt better, everyone else came up to my room again. My dad came in to grab me and met everyone. I hugged everyone goodbye and left. Just got into dad's car right now. I should be home by 3 am.*

It was about 9.30 pm. Dad was driving alongside the river that I had watched from my window on Friday morning. The reflection of the lights from the lampposts rippled slightly against the darkened water. A couple were walking, hand in hand, along the riverside. It was, truthfully, a very romantic place. I would have to bring Jake here one day if I could handle returning.

My dad had connected his phone, so he could play music through the speaker. The voice of Roger Daltrey singing, *Baba O'Riley*, filled the car; one of my favourite songs.

"Thank you for coming to get me," I told my dad. How many times have I apologised and thanked people this weekend? Surely I'd broken a world record by now?

"Well, when I got off the phone to the nurse, your mum and I were pretty much like, 'Okay, which one of us is driving down to get her?' so that was that," he replied, nonchalantly.

"Imagine mum trying to make this drive."

"Exactly." Dad laughed.

"But, like, we could have stayed the night, or rested a bit before continuing, your knees must be in agony," I lamented, desperate to have some validation for the guilt I felt.

"My knees are fine, we'll stop off a couple of times at service stations and get some food." Dad did not give in. "Plus," he added, "we have 'the Who'."

I nodded. "A wise musical selection."

I felt particularly snug in the passenger's seat. I had the pillow tucked behind my head, and the duvet wrapped around me. It was a comforting warmth as I watched the dusky English countryside roll past. As Baba O'Riley became Pinball Wizard, my dad threw me a quick glance.

"You're probably sick of people asking you this, but how are you?"

"At the moment, I'm fine."

That wasn't completely a lie. In the car, with my dad, it felt like time had stopped; just for a moment. Nothing else mattered for now.

"Whenever anyone asks me how I am, and I can't be arsed answering, I just tell them I'm tickety-boo." Dad's inflation rose toward the end of the sentence, as he did an overly fake cheerful voice. "Nobody questions the term tickety-boo."

"It is a fantastic term." I agreed.

"How sick are you of getting asked why you did it?"

"So sick of it! Because there isn't just one single event that made me think 'well here we go, I'm off!'," I spoke with a great deal of passion, "it's a build-up of so many things, I've had depression for years!"

Dad nodded sympathetically, "That's what people just don't get about depression; you don't need a cause to have the symptoms."

My dad was an incredibly open person. I could talk with him freely, perhaps more so as he has faced his own personal mental health difficulties. Unlike my well-meaning friends, my dad came from a place of direct understanding.

I never asked for details about my dad's history, nor would I expect him to share them with me. All I knew was that he'd faced depression, and had been in counselling.

"The hospital made me meet with a therapist type person, and he said because I'm going to Scotland there wasn't really a point in him being there cause he couldn't set anything up for me, and I'd have to speak to my GP when I get home," I explained, "but he still made me speak to him."

"That's pants," Dad said, shaking his head. That was his catchphrase. If an action figure of my dad was ever released, that's what it would say when you pulled the string on the back. "Now you need to go home and sort out aftercare all by yourself."

"Yeah, pretty much." I sighed.

A pleasant silence fell through the car for about ten or fifteen minutes. That was another good thing about my dad. There was never a need to fill the space with mindless talking. You could just nicely co-exist. My quiet contemplation was broken by Jake texting.

JAKE: *Are you going home or coming to mine?*

HEATHER: *Can I come to yours?*

JAKE: *I was hoping you'd say that.*

"I'm glad you were there to defend me about the tidgy puds." I grinned. "They never believed me."

"Tidgy puds are absolutely the right terminology!"

I smiled again, settling into my seat. It was lightly raining, and the drops on the window were almost illuminated by the lights of cars and streetlamps. I wasn't sure where we were. Truthfully, I probably wouldn't know where I was until we were back in East Kilbride, which was still easily five and a half hours away.

Nights like this made me particularly resentful that I was banned from driving. Sorry, not *banned,* just *unable to drive until I go twelve months without a seizure.* I had a doctor tell me off once for using the term, *banned.*

Nonetheless, a rainy, quiet night always brought forward my desire to finally get behind the wheel again. On nights when my depression is peaking, and I'm lying at home in bed, with my thoughts spiralling out of control, I would love nothing more than to just jump in the car and drive away. Sail down some empty country roads, blasting music, singing and crying. Maybe even making a late-night trip to a 24-hour shop, which somehow always seems more exciting at 2 am than it does at 2 pm.

I know a lot of people haven't learned to drive, and many of them never will, but I could drive. And I got that taken away, and sometimes, just sometimes, I get nostalgic thinking about the freedom I had. It was easier to run away from your feelings if you were driving, after all.

The awful bile that is the song, *Boris the Spider*, abruptly broke my thoughts.

"What a bloody shit song," I moaned.

"The only bad song they ever did," Dad echoed my disdain.

Yet, we never skipped it. It was almost traditional now. We had to plunder through the song we hated the most to earn the right to listen to the others. But we never failed to comment on how terrible it was.

Music was always held in very high regard in my family. Some of my earliest memories were of Saturday mornings. I'd be sitting at the breakfast table, eating my toast, and getting prepared to go to all my Saturday morning clubs, whilst my mum and dad would be pottering about, getting ready for the day.

And, every single time, the avant-garde noise of, *the Velvet Underground & Nico*, would fill the house. Each Saturday morning, without fail.

I glimpsed at my dad, who was hate-singing, *Perhaps he's dead, I'll just make sure*.

"How was Mum, when you both found out?" I asked.

"Upset, naturally," Dad answered, "but mostly we were just worried about getting you home."

"Yeah," I exhaled slowly, concentrating my gaze back out the window. I doubted that my dad had been entirely truthful, but that was to be expected.

177

"You know you can tell us anything, right? I know we are your parents, so you might not want to, but you can. Don't think we'll get angry or upset with you, we'd rather just know everything." Dad briefly looked over to me.

"Yeah, I know, but this felt like something entirely different. I didn't even tell Jake until Saturday, or Leigh until Sunday. Even then, Jamie had to phone Jake and Olivia told Leigh."

"I mean before that. If you had told us how you felt Thursday or Friday, one of us could have been down by the next day to stay with you over the weekend."

"I know, but I didn't tell anyone. Suicide is completely different," I tried to explain.

"I know, I know, I just don't want you to think you can't tell us anything."

"Alright, yeah, thank you."

"The way I see it," Dad said, rather earnestly, "every day you wake up, you've won the day before. When you wake up, you're saying to the day before that you beat it. You beat Friday. When you wake up tomorrow, you'll have conquered today."

I smiled softly. "I like that."

"Even if you've done nothing, and you've stayed in bed all day, you still woke up. And, as your dad, I would quite like you to keep waking up, please," he said cheerily, but I knew what he meant.

I laughed. "At least I know I'm allowed to stay in bed all the time now."

"That's the only highlight of depression, you don't need to leave your room." He chuckled.

The next hour passed, and I felt like I was stuck in a repeating loop. The roads looked the same, the night sky was still dark, and every couple of seconds a beacon of light from a car or lamp post flooded my vision. Even the songs had begun repeating. The only real notice of time passing, bar, of course, the clock, was the moon rising. It was a full moon, illuminating its own special spot in the sky. I'm sure there would have been a sprinkle of stars, but we were no longer on the empty country roads, so I couldn't see them.

Regardless of what the English night sky could produce for me tonight, nothing could compare to the view I saw on my first trip away with Jake.

We had only been together about seven or eight months, and we were only going three hours up north to Oban. It was during that lull between our birthdays, in which Jake was already eighteen and I was still seventeen. Yet, we had felt incredibly adult, being away from home for five days, with no adult supervision, for the first time.

We had a top-floor flat, immediately overlooking the horseshoe bay. The flat in question used to be a printing press office and was converted to be a small getaway for visitors. There was a cosy sun nook, with three high windows, offering a beautiful view of the water. There was even a wooden table and chairs so you could sit and enjoy the view.

However, that wasn't the scene I was reminiscing about in the passenger seat of my dad's car.

On our first night in Oban (or was it the second?), we clambered up the steep incline to McCaig's Tower. The tower began construction in 1897 but stopped being built in 1902 when the commissioner died. So only the outer walls of the tower remained, with the inside being transformed into a public garden.

However, it was about 10 pm on a weekday, so the entire area was empty bar us. We proceeded to climb up the granite stairs to the top of the walls, and despite being grossly out of shape and very exhausted, it was worth it.

You could see the whole of Oban from this one point. The entirety of the town was lit up below us by street lights, pubs and restaurants, and homes that hadn't turned off for the night. However, the view wasn't completely luminescent, and the individual streets were still tucked away under a sheet of darkness. You could see our rental flat, and the pier, where all the smaller boats bounced on top of low-level water. And beyond that, you could see the islands of Kerrera, Lismore and Mull.

We were only a few hours from home, and we were only twenty minutes uphill in a town with a population of around 25,000 people. But we felt like we were on top of the world.

I was trying to cherry-pick the good memories to fill my journey home, before I was hit with the reality of reliving this weekend continuously for doctors and therapists, maybe for the rest of my life.

Maybe in some stupid, poetic way, I could try and view my life as the scenery of that night in Oban. Everything was hidden under a cloak of darkness, but every now and then, a burst of light comes through.

I inwardly snorted at my ridiculousness. Metaphors are beautiful when you're writing, but do fuck all in the way of bettering mental health. At least, my mental health anyway. To each their own, I was in no position to judge. I just didn't appreciate using pretty words to try and combat a debilitating mental disease.

"There's a service station ahead, want to pull over?" Dad pointed at a sign, which was yelling out to us to turn left should we choose.

"Yeah, I need to pee." I sat up, fixing my hair. "Had my own weight in fluids pumped into me, can't stop going to the toilet. I want food too."

"Yeah, I could go a sandwich right now," Dad said, pulling into a space, "but we'll just grab stuff to eat on the drive, let's not waste time sitting about."

"Are you sure? Your legs…" I raised an eyebrow.

"I'm fine," Dad insisted.

I was surprised at his perseverance, because stepping out of the car after nearly two hours was a strange sensation, and I had to shake my foot to get some blood running. The man was either made of steel or didn't want to show any discomfort in front of his arguably worse-off daughter.

Service stations hold the same novelty to me that 24-hour shops do. There was an otherworldly atmosphere to it all; the dimmed lights, the minimal noise, unusual shops open past normal hours and staff trying to stay awake. The handful of customers you bump into in these types of places were of a different variety to the average person you pass; they're all doing their own journeys. Although, I doubted many of them were a father-daughter duo returning from England after a failed suicide attempt.

Nonetheless, service stations and 24-hour stores were in their own, timeless bubble of the universe. I would include hotels and airport bars in that bracket too. No past or future; only the present.

Perhaps I was being too poetic about a simple service station.

I ran some water over my face whilst in the bathroom, then put my glasses back on as I glanced at myself in the mirror. It wasn't a pretty sight by any means, I was pale and haggard but at least it was better than how I looked Friday night. My hair had long since dried but was flattened from the car journey. I touched the sleeve of my cardigan, feeling the thickness of the bandage underneath. My thighs were aching slightly under my clothes, but it was bearable.

I regrouped with my dad in the WH Smith that always seemed to be found in these sorts of places. I wandered over to the meal deal section, running my finger over a bookshelf as I passed by. The texture and smell of a new book always comforted me, but I could never figure out why. I would have to remember to pick up some new ones over the next few days. I'd need something to keep me busy until I was back in college – whenever that was.

I had just sat back down in the car and heard the click of my seat belt buckling in when Jake texted me.

JAKE: *I'm trying to stay up until you get here, but it's proving very difficult, ha-ha.*

HEATHER: *Babe, that's insane, don't do that. Just set an alarm for around 3 am. I should be at yours by then. You can just nip out and collect me, then we can go to sleep together.*

JAKE: *Are you sure?*

HEATHER: *Obviously. I'm just in the car. So there is no need for you to be up right now. Just set an alarm and keep your phone volume up in case I need to phone.*

JAKE: *Okay, if you're sure. I love you so much, I can't wait to see you in a few hours.*

HEATHER: *I love you too. It feels like it's been ages.*

"Would you be okay to drop me off at Jake's?" I asked my dad, realising I had forgotten to mention it sooner.

"Certainly, I thought you'd be doing that anyway. Is he staying up or has he set an alarm so he'll wake up nearer the time?"

Sometimes, one of my parents will say something and I'll have a crystallising moment where I think "*Ah! That's where I got it from!*" This was one of those moments.

"He said he was trying to stay up, but I thought that was daft, I told him to set an alarm." I pulled open the packet of a cheese sandwich, taking a bite of it. It was fine, as far as sandwiches go, but had that overwhelming refrigerated chill that all store-bought meal deals had. Plus, the grated cheese was spilling over my blanket. I admired my dad's ability to eat with one hand, and drive flawlessly with the other.

"How was Jake this weekend?" Dad asked in between bites.

"As expected, I suppose. Jamie said he was quite stoic when he phoned him."

"Ah, that's a guy thing though."

"Maybe, yeah. But he has been lovely. Jake always knows what to say or do. And he is fine with me using humour too." I was lucky at just how well my boyfriend knew me.

"If you don't laugh you'll cry, as I always say," Dad said, sounding wise.

Ah! That's where I got it from, I thought.

"EDDIE!" my dad yelled, making me jump a little.

"Damn it!" I groaned, in mock frustration.

"With a journey this long, we're going to get well into double points for this."

183

Eddie, was a game my parents invented long ago before I was born. It was simplistic in its rules, yet somehow very competitive. You had to be on a car journey (the length of the journey was not important). Whenever you see an Eddie Stobart truck, the first person to yell "Eddie!" gets a point. If you see an Eddie Stobart truck with two trailers, you yell "Double Eddie!" first to get two points. However, should you incorrectly call an "Eddie", by, for example, wrongly identifying a truck, then you lose a point. By the end of the journey, the passenger with the most points wins. You gained absolutely nothing from winning, bar glory and bragging rights. Until the next journey, that is.

My family had some peculiar traditions.

"Your mum asked me if I thought the gifts you left for us were 'goodbye' presents," Dad said. It was phrased as a sentence, rather than a question, but I answered regardless.

"Overall, no, it wasn't," I rotated my hands as I spoke. I was quite an animated speaker. I usually used my arms and hands to punctuate sentences.

Dad didn't respond, giving me more room to explain.

"I knew I would be in England for two weeks, so I just wanted to do a nice thing, as a surprise," I explained. I had left a present for my mum and dad on my bed, each gift bag labelled, for them to find during my absence.

I had left a chestnut-scented candle for my mum, and some sweets for Dad. It wasn't much, but after what I did, it probably seemed like a heavily weighted gesture from me.

I had been so absorbed in the past week, that I had forgotten I had done that for them.

"When I flew to England, it wasn't my intention to attempt. But then I began realising that this would be the best

184

opportunity. I don't know, it's hard to explain, but the combination of trying to handle my usual emotions at an escalated level, and being presented with a weekend to myself, it just began to fit together."

"At least it wasn't planned extremely far ahead, it was mildly impulsive."

"Yeah, I suppose." But on the inside, I was thinking, *still ended up in the same boat though.*

Silence fell, yet again, in the car. I rested my head on the pillow. What time was it? About 11:30 pm, apparently. I wasn't one for sleeping in cars, but my eyes felt heavy regardless. If I had still been at the hotel, with everyone, I would likely be in bed, ready for a 7 am start the next day. I probably wasn't going to be having early starts for a while now, at least.

I yawned, so wide it felt like I was unhinging my jaw.

"You want to have a kip?" Dad offered, noticing. I shook my head.

"I don't like sleeping in cars."

Dad looked like he was about to say something, but burst out with "Bloody hell!" instead.

In front of us was a monstrous traffic jam; car after car sitting, at a complete stand-still. I sat up, stretching my neck in an attempt to see the front of the queue, but I couldn't. It almost seemed endless.

"Jesus Christ," I echoed my dad's bewilderment.

We were on a motorway that was slowly leading into a town or city. There was no point in me trying to guess where we were. The congestion was only on the left lane, which I pointed out to my dad.

"Must be construction," Dad thought aloud, "so they're filtering everyone through on the one side."

"We're going to be here for ages," I groaned. The journey was already long enough, and this hold-up would continue on indefinitely. Why was there so much traffic at 11.30 pm on a Sunday?

Dad looked like he was deep in his thoughts. I said nothing, resigning myself to the added inconvenience in front of us. I wanted to be more annoyed, but my emotions were spent. I just had to accept it.

"I wonder if I could drive down the right lane, and someone can let me in further ahead?" my dad asked, hypothetically.

"That's so risky." I laughed. "Dare you."

Dad laughed, and pulled out of the seeming limitless line of cars, into the empty right-hand lane. This was an exaggeration, but for a brief moment, I did not think the traffic jam would end. Maybe I had died and this was my purgatory; being stuck in a gridlock for all eternity with a leg cramp.

I wasn't sure if this would work. What if the road ahead was blocked? What if there were police or construction workers? What if we got stuck at a cordon and had to wait for an age before some kind of driver let us back into the left lane?

During a time when I was facing all the serious issues that I had going on, I was more concerned about a traffic jam. How very typical of me.

Then, suddenly, we were out into the open road. At the end of the lane, Dad managed to pull back into the left somehow. I put it down to some sort of fatherly superpower. Regardless, we were back to making the progress we had been making beforehand, albeit a bit slower, as we trundled through whatever town we were in next.

I yawned heavily, yet again.

Monday

"I'm worried I've fucked all this up," I blurted out, surprising myself a little bit in the process too.

"What do you mean?" Dad asked, turning right at a small roundabout. It was the sort of one that was just white and painted on. Or, as my family called it, a *bird shit roundabout*.

"With college. I already dropped out of university, and now I clearly cannot handle this. Seriously considering dropping this whole media thing and becoming a librarian, or something. Something related to what I like, but not as intense." I sighed.

"You know your mum and I will support you in doing whatever you want. We honestly don't care, as long as you're happy. And whatever you do, we know you will do your best."

I knew this was the same old speech every parent gave their kid, but I knew that my dad was being sincere. I believed him, and I believed in my parents' unconditional support of me.

"Thank you." I hoped that the depth of my gratitude came across in those two words.

"Plus, you're a fighter. You always have been. Do you remember when you were in the nursery?" Dad asked, curiously.

Suddenly, we turned a corner too sharply, I swayed to the side and reached out to balance myself on the dashboard. Dad apologised.

"No, what happened when I was in the nursery?" I asked, readjusting myself.

"You were on the school's pupil council. Despite being in nursery, you were already on the upper school council."

"I don't remember this." I raised my eyebrow.

"Yup. And you only fought for one thing: for strawberry milk to be sold in the cafeteria on a Friday," Dad said this with such warmth in his voice, "and you won."

I laughed. "So that's my legacy. Where's my Nobel prize?"

"Exactly, and I'm guessing you don't remember your first day of primary school?"

"No, what did I do then?"

"Well, parents were meant to come in with you on your first day, but you turned around and told your mum that you didn't need her, and not to come in with you."

"I bet she loved that."

I yawned. Only an hour had passed, making it roughly 12.30 am on Monday. At least we were over the hump; the never-ending weekend had technically ended, even if it didn't feel like it had.

"Can you pull over at the next service station? I need to pee," I said lazily, ending the sentence with another none-too-flattering yawn.

"Yup."

I sat the pillow in the nook between my shoulder and neck, leaning against the window. I felt the gentle bumping as the car rolled forward continuously. I pulled the duvet up, hiding

189

my body under it so I looked like nothing more than a head. I had already kicked off my shoes again, and had my legs crossed; right leg over the left leg. It was the most comfortable I had been thus far.

I closed my eyes, honing in on the lyrics, *how do you think he does it? I don't know! What makes him so good?*

"He plays by sense of smell," I mumbled, sleepily, "you actually mention it in the song, Roger."

I heard my dad smirking lowly.

I shut my eyes. I wasn't expecting to fall asleep; I never could when travelling. There was too much motion. Plus, unless I was in a darkened room next to someone I was fairly comfortable with, I did not like falling asleep in front of somebody. Even my dad.

I yawned again and buried my face into the pillow. It felt smooth and soft, against my skin. Skin that had probably broken out in a disgusting flurry of spots due to stress.

But it smelled fresh. Newly washed. And it smelled like home.

***

I woke up with a start, sitting up and looking around hurriedly. Yes, I was still in the car. Yes, Dad was still next to me, driving.

"For someone who doesn't sleep in cars, you were pretty out of it," Dad said, acknowledging my sudden awakening.

"I fell asleep?" I said, in disbelief.

"I have *never* done that before."

"You've been out of it for about an hour and a half," Dad added, seemingly nonchalant, "it's 2 am right now."

"No way." I shook my head. I felt sweaty and could feel my hair sticking to my cheek where I had been pressed up against the pillow.

"We've passed three service stations, but I didn't want to wake you up."

"What a week. I'm trying all sorts of new things." I chuckled to myself at my shit, dark humour.

"Well, good timing, because there is a station up ahead and I think it'll be our last one; we only have an hour to go," Dad remarked.

Taking my nod as a request to pull in, Dad turned left at the next roundabout. The Satnav, which was programmed to take us home, began beeping at us furiously, not accepting this minor detour. I reached forward and turned it off. We wouldn't be needing it until we got back onto the road anyway.

I slipped my shoes back on and stood out of the car. I wobbled slightly as the blood rushed back into my feet. It was a chilly night, and the cold air hit my face in a welcoming way. Especially after sweating in the car for hours.

By the time we emerged from the service station, I was wide awake, and armed with a can of juice; diet Dr Pepper.

I could almost hear my friends collectively moaning and saying, "That isn't juice!"

My usage of the term 'juice' brought with it as much controversy as the term 'tidgy pud'. Again, for no particular reason, I used the term 'juice' for all manner of drinks, whether it be fizzy, diluent, or fruit. I guess I just don't like being held back by dictionary definitions and prefer to play fast and loose with the English language. Well, that's my excuse anyway. But this, for once, wasn't just a 'Heather thing', as most people I knew in Scotland also did this.

Once, whilst in England for college, I opted to stay in class during a lunch break. Jamie had asked if I wanted anything grabbed whilst he went to the shops, and I asked for juice. When he returned, he placed a bottle of orange juice with pulp in front of me.

I had blinked at him slowly, before saying, "What is this?"

"Juice," was the answer given.

"I meant something like Fanta or Coke."

"Then why did you say juice? You should have said a fizzy drink."

"Juice covers everything."

"It really doesn't. Plus, you like orange juice."

"Not with pulp."

"The pulp is the best bit."

"I'm judging you so much right now," I said, shaking my head at him, "it's like drinking bile."

I smiled to myself as I replayed the conversation in my head. I was going to miss those ridiculous debates (that I always ended up losing) whilst I was at home recovering. But I was certainly not going to miss orange juice with pulp.

My dad and I did not talk much during the last hour of our journey. Anything that had to be said had been said. Our energy was spent.

Slowly, I began recognising places as we got closer and closer to home. The theme park was a half-hour from home, where I had once gone with Jake and he accidentally slammed his hand on a duck that he thought was a statue. The motorway leading into East Kilbride that I used to take my driving lessons on. The supermarket that Jake worked at. The shopping centre with the McDonald's that my ex-girlfriend had broken up with me in and left me crying into my large fries. My pharmacy where I collected my anti-depressants and anti-seizures. The roundabout, where if you went straight through, you'd reach my house, and if you went left, you would reach Jake's.

I heard the beeping of the indicator as dad turned left. I began to pull my shoes back on for the final time. I tied my laces clumsily, feeling a small pit of anxiety in my stomach. I wondered what Jake would be like.

It was 2.50 am when we pulled outside his house. He wouldn't be awake yet.

"I wonder where we would be right now if you hadn't managed to avoid that traffic jam." My voice was slightly hoarse, after not talking in a while. I cleared my throat; feeling the scratching on the inside.

"We'd still be a couple hours out." Dad approximated. "So, when can we expect you home?"

"In a few days. I just want to spend a bit of time with Jake, it won't feel as intense with him."

"Don't be sorry, I get it. Is your lecturer going to be in touch and tell you what is happening with college?"

"Yeah, she will, I don't know what is happening with that right now." I yawned.

I pulled my phone out to call Jake and wake him up. It had quite a low charge, and a few notifications I was going to ignore until I woke up from what I hoped would be a twelve-hour sleep, minimum. To be honest, I would have accepted a temporary coma, I was that fatigued.

"Hmm?" I hear Jake sleepily mumble down the phone.

"I'm outside," I whispered into the phone, not wanting to deafen him.

"Hmm, okay," I heard Jake sitting up before he hung up the phone.

"Was he still asleep?" Dad asked lightly, smiling a little under the light of the lamppost that shone through the front window of the car.

"Yeah, I feel really guilty." I laughed. There was a moment's pause before I said, "Thank you, Dad. I appreciate this so much. You must be exhausted. Are you going into work tomorrow?"

"Nope, I will be sleeping until late afternoon at least," Dad said cheerily, "don't thank me, I would have driven anywhere I needed to pick you up."

"Next time, I'll make sure I'm somewhere nicer, like Paris."

Dad chuckled, before yawning.

I saw the hall light flickering on from Jake's house, and saw his silhouette moving down the stairs.

"There he is." I unbuckled my seat belt. With the music off, it was a surprisingly loud noise. I felt my stomach relax after being held behind the polyester. I wondered if I would have a mark on my skin from it. It wouldn't be the worst mark I've had recently.

I popped open the car door as Jake opened his front door, accidentally synchronising. Dad reached forward, lightly pressed a button, and I heard the noise of the car boot opening.

I stood and stretched as wide as I possibly could without bursting apart, groaning as if I were sixty years older than I was. I would be perfectly fine not having a car journey for the rest of my life.

Jake joined my side as I pulled the suitcase out. The weight was more noticeable than before, likely due to how physically weak I felt. Jake took it from my hands.

"Thank you," I said, sheepishly.

I fumbled my way back to the front of the car, shutting my door and leaning in through the open window to talk to Dad again.

"Thank you so much, I'll sort out a game plan tomorrow," I said, sounding like a broken record.

"Okay." Dad turned his head to my right. "Hi, Jake, sorry to wake you up."

"Thank you for dropping Heather off." I could tell he was stifling a yawn. The conversation felt uncomfortably formal, which wasn't typical for them. My Dad thought Jake was brilliant, and vice versa. Considering the abnormal circumstances, however, I guess neither of them knew what to say. They were the father and the boyfriend of the suicidal girl.

"I love you, Dad, I hope you get a lot of sleep." I stood, my lower back mildly throbbing with pain.

"Alright, keep in touch, okay? I'll see you in a few days, we can talk more then." Dad started the car up, before slowly driving back down the hill, throwing a wave our way.

It was a pleasant and simple goodbye. That was all I needed. Much like I had drained my desire to ever be in a car again, I was completely finished with emotionally charged goodbyes. My dad clearly understood that. Plus, at 3 am after a six-hour drive (and twelve hours for my dad), I think both of us were just desperate to get to bed.

To get to Jake's house, you had to trail down a small set of concrete stairs. It was pleasant and cooled during the summer months, but very hazardous during the winter. I had slipped on ice and landed on my arse more times than I care to mention.

The night was as cold and chilled as it had been in England, which was oddly comforting to me. As if part of it had come home with me. I'd miss my classmates, but at least we were under the same sky.

Jake had left the door open, so we slipped in.

"Are your parents home?" I whispered, just in case.

"No, they're at work, don't worry."

"Ah, okay." I returned to my normal volume.

Jake's mum was a nurse, whilst his dad was a care worker. Having both been in their fields for so long, they had some say in their shift pattern, and they used this leverage to synchronise their night shifts, allowing them the same days off. And gifting Jake and I with an empty house every few days.

Jake turned off the hall light, then went upstairs, almost leaping. He was probably in a hurry to get back to bed. I darted up behind him. I'm not afraid of the dark, in fact, I'm a 'lights off during sex' kind of girl.

Yet, a small part of my childhood fear of monsters that grab you in the night still lingered. I hated going up the stairs when I couldn't see properly.

Jake's room was as dark as the night we had just walked through. I flicked the light switch on, hearing my sleepy boyfriend groan in mild protest.

It felt like an age since I had last been in the comfort of these four walls. I still remembered how bare Jake's room had been the first time I had visited; a bed, a television, a desk, a small set of drawers, brown wallpaper, and laminate flooring.

Several years in, however, and it had become a homely den, with evidence of our lives together all over the walls.

Over his desk was a collage of photos, tickets, cards and receipts; telling the story of all our adventures together. There was a map of Oban, which our landlord had given to us on our first trip away together. We had hung a photo of one of our BBQs, as the Struggle all balanced on the splintered fence. Under it were ferry tickets to Belfast, and a photo of Gaby, Ben, Sam, Jake and I outside the zoo, beaming under the sun.

A photo from Jake's cousin's wedding was also pinned up; with Jake looking handsome in his suit, whilst I stood next to him in a black jumpsuit, my arm wrapped around his. Next to tickets from my band concerts was a photo of us on the beach, where Jake had taken me on my 20th birthday, and next to that was a photo of us with his niece, when we took her to the arcade. A framed movie poster of, *Stand By Me*, hung next to the tickets from a comic book exhibit we went to. There were even some photos from a booth, with Graham, Jake and I when Jake came to England with me during college time.

In the corner of the room was a tank. I couldn't see too clearly into it at the moment as the internal lighting was off. Not that I needed to see into it as I already knew what was there. It was a bearded dragon, a rather extravagant gift I had gotten Jake for his 19th, who was lovingly named Haggis. She hated me. And on top of the tank was a pile of books; mostly mine.

Jake put my suitcase down and turned to hug me wordlessly. We stood for about thirty seconds in our silent embrace. The familiarity of his body, his smell, and the feeling of his breath on my neck, relaxed the tension I was holding. I was home.

"Can we go to bed?" I whispered into his ear.

"And we can talk in the morning?"

"Yeah, of course." Jake pulled back, staring at me for a moment as if he was trying to soak all the details of my face in.

I pulled off my trousers, before unhooking my bra and pulling it out of my sleeve. I didn't have the energy to open my case and pull my pyjamas out. I collapsed onto the bed in my t-shirt and underwear. The underwear I dawned wasn't particularly attractive; I sported high-waisted, black pants. It tucked my disgusting stomach in. Comfort over sex appeal. If it bothered Jake, he never mentioned it. I rolled onto my back, and looked up at him, smiling gently. It was good to see his face. Looking at him was the most reassuring thing to me. If home was a person, it would be Jake.

However, he wasn't looking at me. He was staring at my thighs and arms stoically. In my burst of exhausted delight at seeing him, I had forgotten to warn Jake about the damage.

"Babe," he breathed. He didn't finish his sentence, but I knew what he was thinking.

"It doesn't hurt." I tried to reassure him. "My thighs are a bit nippy because they're not covered, but my arms just feel like there is some pressure from the bandages."

Jake didn't say anything.

"Hey, at least it wasn't you in hospital this time." I laughed delicately, trying to bring a bit of light-heartedness into the situation.

"I'd have preferred that," Jake said, sighing.

Jake had Crohn's Disease. I remember when he had told me. We had been walking back from Ryan's house, after a long day of being filmed shooting balloons. We had only known each other for about two weeks and hadn't begun dating yet. By then, however, I already felt strongly drawn toward him. He was intoxicating.

I hadn't experienced the effects of one of his flare-ups until around eight months into dating when he had been admitted to the hospital. I remember bursting into his room and sobbing so hard that I was completely incoherent. Jake was sitting in bed, dawning a hospital gown, with an IV drip in one arm. He looked pale but began laughing when he saw me.

"Babe, don't cry! I'm fine!" he had declared.

If Jake's health ever worried him, he didn't show it. Perhaps part of him had accepted that he was always at risk of a flare-up, that remission only lasted so long, and that a lifetime of medication faced him.

Perhaps it was that "Well it isn't going anywhere, so let's deal with it", attitude that let him laugh when he was in an A&E room yet again.

Perhaps he didn't want to let on how scared he was.

By then, this sort of crisis was routine. He would use this time to catch up on school work, and as he got older, university work. He knew the staff by name and could have walked the hospital corridors blindfolded. For me, however, this was my first time seeing the man I loved sick. Not just some mild cold, but frighteningly sick. It was incredibly overwhelming.

He stayed in the hospital for approximately four days that time. Since then, he has been hospitalised three other times for on average, a week.

The second time was the day before my high school prom. The night of my prom was spent in a private hospital room, eating Quavers and moaning that there were only two hours of visiting time for us to be together. I didn't mind; I would have chosen Jake over prom a million times over.

After Jake was discharged, my mum gave me money to take the Struggle out for a fancy dinner. A 'make-up prom' if you will. We would all dress up, and go into one of the posh restaurants in Glasgow. That, too, was cancelled when Jake was hospitalised again.

The most recent, and possibly the most difficult time, was last Christmas when Jake spent Boxing Day through to the 2nd of January in hospital. His New Year's Eve was celebrated by being alone in a hospital ward, trying to avoid the elderly gentlemen with dementia in the bed across from him, who kept climbing into next to him.

I wonder if Jake was feeling the exact same things I felt whenever I saw him at his weakest.

"Come lie in bed." I patted the space next to me. Jake turned the light off, before collapsing next to me.

"I felt so useless," he said unexpectedly, "I was so far away, and I couldn't do anything to help. It should have been me driving down to get you, too."

I ran my hand through Jake's hair. I had never realised I had a thing for gingers until I met him. We were lying on our sides, facing each other. I could make out his face even in the darkness.

"You spoke to me, and kept me company. You spoke to Jamie for me. And now that I'm home you'll basically be my carer whilst I play the role of a useless mess. Plus, we both know your car could not have handled that journey." I grinned.

"Yeah, that's true." Jake ran a finger down the bandage on my arm lightly so as not to pull it apart.

"I'm going to be disfigured. Deformed as fuck. I've ruined myself."

"No, you haven't. We will look after it. Creams, or whatever, to fade it. Even tattoos, eventually, if you want."

"Will you still fancy me if I'm scarred?"

"Of course, I'll always fancy you."

"Wish I could say the same, but you did go through that period where you had a buzz cut," I joked.

"Oi!" Jake exclaimed in mock anger.

"I need to sleep, I'm about to pass out here." As if to prove my point, I yawned loudly, and unattractively.

"You must be pretty done in. Sleep as long as you need. When you wake up, we will order pizza and watch trashy television, and you can talk about everything as much or as little as you want. We take this at your speed, not other peoples."

"Thank you, Jake, I love you."

"I love you too."

I rolled over, turning away from my sweet boyfriend. It felt exceedingly euphoric to lie down. I wanted to be horizontal forever. I never wanted to sit up again. I could add that to the list of things I never wanted to do again, alongside car journeys and emotional goodbyes.

The bed shifted as Jake scooted closer to me, wrapping his arm around me. This was something I normally protested; Jake's body soured to impressively high temperatures during the night. Plus, he snored. Loudly. Like a choking wildebeest. But this time I didn't care. It was nice to be held. I felt safe.

It wasn't long before I felt Jake's breath against my neck. He had a knack for falling asleep absurdly quick. I, however, would probably be awake for a little longer, despite how little I had slept the past few days.

I was nervous about what would be happening when I woke up. The weekend would officially be over. I would be out of the limbo that manifested in a blur of hospitals, driving and conversation. The weekend had felt like a month of Sunday afternoons. When I woke up, I would have to figure out what the fuck I was going to do. I would have to speak to Leigh about college, to which I had no idea what was going to happen. I would need to arrange therapy, where I would probably be put on a waitlist indefinitely. I would need to change my medication, as it clearly wasn't working. It would be a time when I would be under constant surveillance and scrutiny. I would need to go home and face my mum, seeing the look on her face after all of this.

And that wasn't even taking into consideration my future. A week from now. A month from now. A year from now. I had loosely talked about it with Marcus, but everything was hanging by a thread. Anything could happen.

Before this weekend, I had felt temporary; like a blip in everyone's life, soon to be forgotten. Now? I felt incredibly permanent. Nothing was going away, and neither was I, and now I need to figure out how to handle that all.

I rolled back over, facing Jake, and watched his body slowly rise and fall as he snored gently. He looked sweet, with his face pressed against the pillow, his hair ruffled, and his mouth slightly open. Four years ago, I didn't even know him, and now I couldn't imagine going a single day without him.

He felt the same about me, and I had forced him to face a future where I might not be there. God, I'd never stop feeling fucking guilty about that.

I sighed, and lay on my back, looking at the popcorn ceiling. Just like I had done on Friday morning. That Friday felt so final, and so long ago.

What do I do with this life I had to see through to the end? I had no fucking clue.

Maybe I could actually get the rest of the tattoos I wanted? Yeah, that could be good. I could get the sunflower, the cocktail glass, the paper aeroplane, the fortune cookie…I could finally cover myself. And, eventually, cover the scars that I'd have.

And piercings too! I could get the nape piercing I'd wanted for years. Jake always winced when I said I wanted the back of my neck pierced, but I might actually get around to doing it now. I wonder if my hair would get caught in it a lot.

I have a pile of books I never got around to reading. Moby Dick, Roots, and what was the other one? *We!* that was it. The daddy of dystopian novels.

I did want to start dying my hair crazy colours again; pink, blue, purple, and green. The whole spectrum, like I used to do when I was in high school. I had been blonde for too long now, I was getting bored of it.

I would need to go visit my mum and dad and hug them tight. Tell them that I loved them and that I was sorry. And thank them for everything. Prove to them I can be a better daughter than my past implied.

I'd also go to visit Gran and Grandpa, and sit and take in all their stories about Wemyss Bay, and their eagerness for an engagement. Listen to Grandpa's awful jokes and Gran's stories about all her friends from her church group, and all her "Guess who died this week?" comments.

I'd go for a drink with the Struggle, soak in all their ridiculous energy, and play drinking games. I'd take those photos with Sam that he promised me and fill up our collection.

I'd lie in bed and hold my cat, and feel her breath as she purred slowly against my arm.

Eventually, I could go back to college too and began to try and repay everyone back for all they did for me. Especially Jamie.

And I'd take Jake on the most incredible dates, and shower him with as much love as I'm capable of pouring out; continually.

I didn't know what was going to happen to me emotionally, for the next while. I'd be all over the place, I'm sure. I was going to need so much therapy and a change in medication. Maybe a complete change in lifestyle.

And working in the future? That seems like an improbability right now. I could barely make it through education. But, I suppose, I would get there in the end. I had to now. I'd tried giving up on myself, so maybe it was time to start believing in me instead. Which was easier said than done, I suppose.

A whole new journey would begin in the morning. The weekend would end.

There was one thing I could at least be certain of. At some point, in years from now, I wouldn't remember this weekend completely. I'd forget the details, and the emotions, hopefully, too. At some point in my life, if this weekend was ever brought up again, I would be able to say, "Oh that? That was sometime in August, years ago. But I'm okay now."

But for now, all I had to do was sleep.